Dedication

To all the authors who took part in the *Possessed by Passion* list run; your hard work and dedication inspire me to do better.

Chapter One

The unmarked black transit vans sat side by side in the Echo Park parking lot, pointed in the direction of the hospital across the street. One of the vans was equipped with weaponry and a cage in the cargo area, while the other was home to all manner of computer equipment, all of which had blinked out when the earthquake aftershock hit.

"How's it looking back there?" the team leader asked the IT guys in the back of the van.

"Systems are coming back online now, Drake."

"As quickly as you can, gents. I need to know if that bitch is still in there." Lionel Drake stared at the hospital across the way. Half of the building was plunged into darkness, while the other half clung to generator power.

Their boss, Spencer Thorn, had dispatched them to capture the newest creature for his collection. They had, though, arrived a little too late, a massive

Salem

John Watson

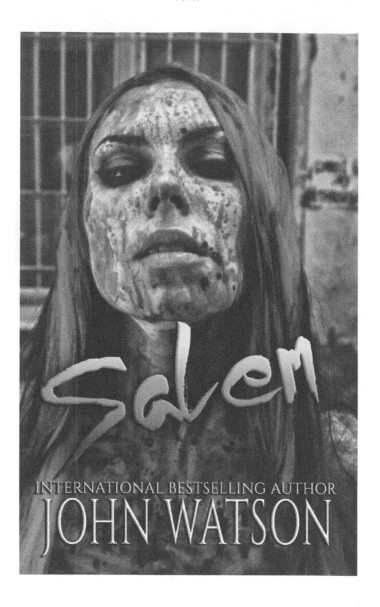

INTERNATIONAL BESTSELLING AUTHOR

JOHN WATSON

earthquake freeing the Aswang from Echo Park Lake. Drake had been all about charging into the hospital and taking the creature by force, but Thorn had told them to stand down. A hospital, even one on the brink of closure, would have witnesses inside, which could potentially kill a stealth operation.

Drake did not feel good about letting innocent people die, but given how much money Thorn threw at him, it became easier to swallow the inevitable civilian casualties. He always imagined that once he left his illustrious military career behind, he would land a private security job. Drake did not expect that he would be getting paid top dollar to hunt down and trap creatures he'd only believed existed in horror movies, yet that is precisely where he had ended up, bagging monsters for an eccentric billionaire's private collection.

"We are back online," one of the IT guys called from the back of the van.

Reaching down, Drake lifted a device that looked like an oversized police radar unit and pointed it at the hospital. The display showed the heat signatures of three humanoid shapes. "We have movement inside. It looks like two human souls and one unidentified."

"Confirmed. That'll be our girl."

"Should we go in?" the driver asked as he fidgeted in his seat.

"Not yet, Rankin." Drake gave the driver a quick sideways glance, concerned that he was going to jump the gun. It was his first time working with the new man, and he did not have a good feeling about him. "I'll tell you what. Go over and talk to Givens in the armory van. Get us the weapons we need for when we do go in."

Rankin hopped out of the van with a quick nod and jogged over to the other vehicle, sliding inside and out of sight in the blink of an eye.

"Is it just me, or is that guy a little too high-strung?"

Turning to look at the IT guys—or the Nerd Patrol, as he called them—Drake pursed his lips. "Don't worry about him. Keep an eye on our girl."

In the beginning, Drake had complained that the Nerd Patrol was an unnecessary addition to his team. He had complained to Thorn that the last thing he needed on a mission was a pair of geeks to babysit, but Bits and Bytes, the codenames they had assigned themselves, had proven to be an invaluable resource on more than one occasion. The fact that they felt the same about Rankin as Drake did confirmed that his feelings about the man were probably correct.

Examining the figures on the scanner, Drake fought the urge to ignore orders and bolt across the street to help the people trapped inside with the creature. Catching movement out of the corner of his eye, he turned to see Rankin step out of the second van, weapons in hand. The man was little more than a shadow figure cutting through the dark, but every single detail came into focus for a moment as an explosion rocked through the second floor of the hospital.

"What the heck was that?" Bits and Bytes cried in unison.

The scanner screen had turned a bright shade of red, the heat of the flames the only reading it could pick up. Drake gave the device a shake and pointed it back at the building, praying it would pick up something from inside the wreckage. He jumped out of the van and almost fell over Rankin, who lay on the ground with an assault rifle pointed at the hospital. "What the fuck are you doing?" Drake asked, planting a boot in the man's side.

"We are under attack."

"How do you figure that? The people inside that building have no idea we are here. They are fighting for their goddamn lives against that…that…thing in there."

Jumping quickly to his feet, Rankin pressed in tight against Drake till they were almost nose to nose. "Don't talk down to me. EVER."

Snatching the weapon out of Rankin's hand, Drake pushed the man in the chest, sending him backward, arms pinwheeling. "I'll talk to you any way I want. I'm in charge here, and you would do well to shut up and listen."

Fists clenched, Rankin fumed, glaring at Drake with evil intent in his eyes. He took a hesitant step forward, like someone testing the ice on a newly frozen pond.

"I will put you down without thinking twice," Drake said, trying to ignore Givens, who had stepped out of the second van and was advancing on Rankin, a baseball bat cocked and ready to swing.

Letting out a roar, Rankin went to make his move, but the loud thump of the bat connecting with his skull ended the attack before it began. Without saying a word, Givens dragged the unconscious man across the tarmac and dumped him into the cage in the back of the van.

"We are going to need that space," Drake said.

"If things go as planned, we'll have the creature tranked and back at the facility before this moron wakes up."

"And if we don't?"

"Then our newest exhibit will have a bite to eat for the ride home. Speaking of which, where is that nasty fucking creature?"

Picking up the weapons, Drake returned to his van, picked up the scanner, and pointed it at the hospital. "What do you see, guys?"

"One heat signature. Human."

"FUCK. Thorn is not going to be pleased," Drake yelled, pounding his fist against the dashboard.

"Hold on," Bytes said. "It's changing."

"What do you mean?"

"I mean that the thing that was human isn't quite so human anymore."

Drake looked at the scanner but needed a bigger display to better understand what was going on. Slipping between the seats, he moved into the back of the van, still pointing the scanner at the building across the street. Staring at the oversized monitor in front of Bits and Bytes, it became clear that what they were looking at was not human.

"How is that possible?" Drake asked, peering at the screen.

"This creature is a shapeshifter, but she may also be, how can I put it, infectious."

"Call me stupid, Bits, but how so?"

"That explosion may have blown her to pieces. If anyone left standing up there ingested her blood or pieces of her flesh, they might well take on her form."

Drake shook his head as he watched the image on the monitor move through the hospital. "Time to move in," he said. The words had barely escaped his lips when a squad of emergency vehicles came tearing down the street, lights flashing and sirens blaring.

"Looks like the cavalry has arrived," Bits said.

With a groan, Drake passed the scanner to Bytes. "Get up front and keep an eye on what's happening. If that thing gets out, let me know right away."

"What are you going to do?"

Clambering out the back of the van, Drake looked back and said, "I'm going to gear up. We are a man down now, so I want to be ready to take that bitch down as soon as we get the opportunity."

Chapter Two

They sat and watched the activity in the hospital parking lot, keeping an eye on the movement of the creature, who had shifted into the guise of one of the first responders. Drake's heart pounded as the adrenaline coursed through his body. Never taking his eyes off the building across the street, he slowed his breathing as he fought to get his nerves under control. He had been in countless battle situations, and while he was always able to remain calm during the fighting, his nerves always felt frayed in the moments before it all went down.

"She's on the move," Bits called from the back of the van. "Moving quickly. My guess is that she is in a vehicle."

Drake tossed the scanner aside and watched as a squad car rolled up to the hospital entrance, stopped for a moment, and then turned onto the street. "Let's roll," he said.

The two vans slid in behind the cop car, keeping far enough back to remain inconspicuous yet close enough to stay with the vehicle should the driver make an unexpected bolt for freedom. That never happened, though, as the cop car glided into a diner parking lot a few minutes after leaving the hospital.

Driving past the diner, Drake took a second to glance inside the brightly lit building, counting five people inside. He knew that there would probably be at least one more person in the kitchen, which meant too many witnesses inside if they stormed in and tried to capture the creature.

Both vans pulled a U-turn and parked across the street from the diner. Drake's radio crackled as Givens spoke. "What now, boss?"

"We wait and take it down when she leaves."

"Roger that."

Bytes moved out of the back of the van, sliding between the seats and plopping himself down in the passenger seat. He pushed his glasses up on the bridge of his nose and coughed nervously. "So, uh, tell me a little more about that thing in there."

"It's an Aswang. A shapeshifter that landed here on a cargo ship filled with illegal Filipino immigrants. The story goes that they captured it and chained it to the bottom of Echo Park Lake over fifty years ago."

"How did it get out? I mean, what are the chances?"

"I'm not sure, but I'm guessing years of earthquakes loosened its bonds. She will be hungry and pissed, so we may well have a fight on our hands. It normally goes after pregnant women and children, but given the circumstances, she may eat whatever is available."

Fidgeting in his seat, Bytes cleared his throat. "So, about that. Do you need our help? We are a man down with Rankin losing his shit."

The sound of the engine cooling ticked loudly in the cabin, sounding like a clock counting down the seconds, waiting for Drake to reply. "Do you know how to fire a weapon?" he asked, never taking his eyes off the diner.

"I've taken some lessons at the range."

"These tranquilizer guns have more of a kick than what you are used to at the range, Bytes," Drake said sternly. "I don't need you sending a dart flying into the ass of a random civilian."

"I can handle it."

Drake sighed before pointing to one of the tranquilizer guns leaning against the passenger door. "Take one of those, but stay behind Givens and me. Only fire that thing if things get out of control, which they shouldn't. Do you understand me?"

"I got it," Bytes said nervously, sounding like a man who instantly regretted the decision he had just made.

The radio sprang to life again as Givens spoke, "Boss, we may have a problem. Advise."

Reaching across Bytes, Drake snatched up his weapon before hopping out of the truck and moving around to the passenger side to get a closer look at the diner. The cop who they had followed there was on his feet at the counter, his body trembling as though having a seizure. While Drake didn't have the best view of the server, he could see that she was scared and that she looked to be very pregnant.

Givens jogged up beside him, hands on the weapons in his holster. "What the fuck is happening?"

"I think she's changing to feed. We need to move now and worry about civilians later." Drake balled his fist and pounded on the door of the van. "Let's roll, Bytes, but remember to stay behind us.

As they ran across the street, the creature shifted from cop to something out of a nightmare, leaping onto the counter, her spear-tipped tongue flashing out of her mouth and catching the server in the stomach.

"Shit. Givens, take out the civilians. I'll handle that nasty fucking bitch."

As they crashed through the diner door, the creature turned to face them, her black eyes narrowing as they raised their weapons.

Givens pulled both guns out of the holster and started firing immediately, the tranquilizer darts hitting each of the diner patrons square in the chest and dropping them before they had a chance to register what was happening.

The Aswang sucked in her tongue, blood dripping off the tip, and threw herself at the server. They fell to the floor and out of sight just as Drake fired. The tranquilizer dart flashed through the greasy black hair of the creature as she fell, catching the short-order cook, who had just stepped out of the kitchen, in the throat. His eyes rolled back in his head as he fell, tongue lolling out the side of his mouth.

Drake and Givens moved towards the flap in the counter as Bytes stood at the diner door, rooted to the spot. As Givens lifted the flap, the server stood, tears streaming down her face as she clutched at her stomach, trying in vain to stop the flow of blood.

"Please don't hurt my baby," she wailed.

Raising a hand, Drake inched forward, trying to get a look behind the counter to see what was happening with the creature. He peered through the crack in the swinging doors leading to the kitchen, which were now held open by the cook's sleeping body.

"That's not the waitress," Givens hissed, nodding at the floor behind the counter.

Craning his neck, Drake peered around the countertop and saw the server's white-sneakered feet poking out from under the cook's prone form.

The Aswang shifted back to her original form as the first dart caught her in the shoulder. She reached across and pulled it out of her wrinkled grey skin, flicking it away as though it were nothing more than a bothersome gnat. She advanced on the men as they continued to fire.

"Huuuuuunnnngrrrry," she hissed as her proboscis shot out of her mouth, the barbed end falling just short of Drake's face.

19

Taking a small step back, Drake calmly hoisted his weapon and fired again. The dart flew through the opening at the tip of the creature's tongue, causing her to stagger backward, arms flailing as her clawed hands sought purchase on the counter as she fell.

The creature lay motionless on the floor, eyes open and staring. Moving forward, Drake kicked at her foot but got no response. He pulled the creature away from the bodies she had fallen on, the server moaning quietly as the weight fell away from her. "Get this nasty piece of work bound and into the van," he said as he moved in to attend to the waitress.

Givens bound the Aswang's hands and feet with twist ties and lifted her over his shoulder with a grunt, shuddering as her slimy flesh touched his neck. "Make yourself useful, Bytes, and get the door for me. Make sure the coast is clear."

Once Givens and Bytes were clear of the building, Drake knelt beside the server and placed his hand on hers, which were covering the ragged wound in her stomach.

"Help me," she whispered. "Please."

Moving her hands to the side, Drake took a look at the wound, hissing at the sight of the damage. Different scenarios ran through his mind in the time it took to blink an eye, but his options narrowed when the small clawed hand reached out from inside the woman's stomach. It was followed by a head covered in lank, straggly black hair. The thing looked like a miniature version of the creature they had just fought, and it brought a stinging stream of bile to the back of Drake's throat.

He quickly glanced at the server's face and could see that she had passed. Drake gently closed her eyelids and turned his attention back to the creature, who was now staring at him and smiling. "Well, look at you. Such an ugly little fuck, but a valuable one. Thorn would pay me a nice bonus if I took you in alive. What do you say to that?"

The infant opened her mouth and hissed, her barbed tongue probing the air.

Drake glared at the child and shuddered as he saw his reflection turned upside down in her dead black eyes. "You know what, munchkin? I make enough money already. Fuck that bonus." Pulling out his handgun, Drake put a bullet between the creature's eyes and then cut her free from the dead waitress's body.

Back at the van, he tossed the child into the cage beside the Aswang and Rankin, who was beginning to come out of his unconscious state with a series of grunts and moans. Drake fired a dart into the team member's body, thinking it better to have him down for the count until they returned to the Thorn facility.

He thumped the side of the van, giving Givens the signal that it was time to leave. Drake climbed behind the wheel of the second van and looked back at the tech guys. "You hanging in there, Bytes?"

"I'm okay. From now on, though, I think I'll stick to computers."

"I think that might be a good idea. Let's go see Thorn. I think he's going to love the latest addition to his collection."

Chapter Three

Drake's eyes fluttered open as the cargo plane hit turbulence on its descent into San Francisco airspace and the private airstrip connected to the Thorn Industries main building. Rubbing his eyes, he peered out the window and watched the downtown buildings slip past, the city awash in lights that turned night into day.

He slid the window cover down and snatched up the radio from the pocket on the seat in front of him. "How are things looking down there, Givens?"

"All the little ones are asleep and dreaming."

"What about Rankin?"

"Still out, but it's a little weird."

"Weird how?"

There was a pause on the other end of the line, small bursts of static punctuating the silence. "That thing is cuddled up to Rankin."

"What do you mean?"

"The bitch is spooning him. It's somewhat romantic," Givens said with a chuckle.

"You are one hundred percent sure she is still out?"

"Like a light. Relax, boss. We are almost home."

Stuffing the radio back in the pocket, Drake slid out of his seat and walked to the back of the plane, where Bits and Bytes sat, hammering away at their laptops. The tech guys usually stayed in their van down in the cargo hold during flights, but Bytes seemed unwilling to spend any more time in the presence of the Aswang.

"What's the word, guys?" Drake asked.

Bytes seemed to ignore the question, choosing instead to focus on the lines of code on his laptop screen. Bits was more open to conversation. "Not bad, boss. Bytes is working on fine-tuning some of our tracking software, and I'm doing some research on our next target."

"Which is?"

"Our field personnel have been looking into stories of an alleged vampire in New Orleans. Not sure yet if he's the real deal or just some guy that likes his meat extra rare."

"What about our target here in town?"

"Still quiet there. If that girl knows what she is, she's keeping it to herself."

"Okay, good. Keep me posted." Drake moved back to his place, holding the tops of the seats for support as the plane banked and made its final approach to the Thorn airstrip. He had barely sat back down when the plane landed with a thump, the engine roaring as the pilot engaged the brakes.

Drake stood at the top of the steps and watched as the ground personnel unloaded the vans from the cargo hold and sped off in the direction of the main building. He bounded down the steps intending to hitch a ride to the warehouse to help with the intake of the creature, but he barely made it off the bottom step before Spencer Thorn appeared as though from out of thin air, arm extended.

"Mister Thorn. Good to see you, sir," Drake said, shaking the billionaire's hand and trying to avoid grimacing at the feel of the ruined appendage.

"Likewise, Lionel. Any problems in bagging my girl?"

"Nothing we couldn't handle, sir. We do need to talk about Rankin, but I will break all of that down when we have our debriefing." Drake eyed the vans as they entered the vast warehouse off in the distance, desperate to get there and make sure that the Aswang made it to her assigned cell with the minimum of fuss.

Maneuvering his powerchair between Drake and the warehouse, Thorn blocked any possible exit. "I'd like to have that meeting now, Lionel. I'm keen to hear more about the beast you captured."

A knot of frustration began to form in Drake's belly, which he tried to swallow down to no avail. "If it's all the same with you, sir, I'd sooner get that thing squared away first."

"Nonsense. Givens can handle it. He has plenty of men at his disposal. I think you have earned a break, so meet me in my office in ten minutes."

"Of course, sir."

***

Givens stood with his back to the freight elevator doors and kept an eye on his men and the prisoners they held captive. Both Rankin and the Aswang were still out cold, but he wanted to make sure they stayed that way before they were locked up.

The elevator descended slowly, no numbers marking their descent. There was only one stop on this trip, which came at the bottom of an elevator shaft that descended a mile or so below ground to a warren of cells where all manner of creatures called home. It was a place that was almost certainly the wet dream of any serious cryptozoologist, but no one except a select few knew anything about Spencer Thorn's extraordinary collection.

The elevator reached its destination and stopped with a muffled thump. Givens turned as the door slid open and made his way to the guard room at the head of a long hallway that stretched off into the distance. Rapping on the glass door, he stepped inside and shook hands with the guard on duty. "Are the inmates behaving, Shane?"

The guard nodded as he scanned a row of monitors on the panel in front of him. "All quiet on the western front. Did everything go to plan in San Fran?"

Givens grunted. "All except for Rankin. Idiot lost his cool and left us a man down. Did you manage to get a cell set up for him like we asked?"

"I did. What do you think Thorn is going to do with him?"

"I wouldn't be surprised if he became the next meal for the meg, but who knows."

Shane threw his head back and laughed. "Sooner him than me. Rankin is in cell number sixteen down the hall. I have cell thirty-eight for our new guest."

"Shit, that's right by Raven," Givens said, suddenly looking nervous.

"That's where Thorn wants it."

"I'm convinced that creepy fucker does this shit to mess with me. Thorn knows I hate being anywhere near her."

Shane shrugged. "I'm just following orders, mate. Are you ready to take them in?"

"Yes. Initiate door opening sequence."

The guard placed his hand on a biometric scanner and punched a code into the keypad beside the screen. Givens repeated the process on a second scanner and watched as the heavyweight door to the facility slid open. He wrinkled his nose as the smell of shit and dead animals used as food wafted out from the cells.

Givens turned just in time to see something fly past his face. Whipping around, he saw the object latch onto Shane's throat and begin to suck loudly. "What the fuck?"

One of the men transporting the prisoners screamed in pain, pulling Givens' attention away from the guard, whose body was beginning to fold in on itself as all the fluids made their way up the feeding tube.

It took Givens a moment to react to what was going on. It was the fountain of blood splashing his face that snapped him back to reality. As he reached for his weapon, the Aswang, which was slowly shifting to look like Rankin, tossed aside one of the guards, his throat torn to shreds by razor-sharp claws as she grabbed for the other.

The real Rankin's eyes fluttered as the tranquilizer wore off, and he stumbled forward, falling into Givens as the creature tore open the other transport guard. Pushing him aside, Givens raised his weapon, but before he could get a shot off, the Aswang grabbed his wrist and twisted it violently. Save for the tongue, which continued to suck the life out of Shane, the creature now looked completely like a grinning, maniacal version of Rankin.

It twisted Givens' wrist again as it dragged him into the long corridor, smiling as it pulled him past cells containing creatures thought to be nothing more than the stuff of myth and legend. Some of them reached through the bars, trying to grab hold of them as they passed, but the Aswang stayed in the middle of the hallway and headed for the cell at the end, which faced down the long corridor.

This one was different from the rest in that it was made entirely of glass, like some sort of oversized killing jar. A woman sat inside, watching the events unfold with a smirk on her face. She stood and moved to the front of the cell, her long black dress hiding her feet and making it look as though she were gliding along the concrete floor. Her bright red hair was long and tucked behind her ears, revealing a high-cheekboned face that would have been at home on the cover of any fashion magazine.

Givens tried to wrestle free of the Aswang, but he screamed as the creature applied more pressure on his wrist, the sound of small bones cracking cutting through the screams and howls of the caged animals.

The red-haired woman pressed her hands against the glass and watched as the thing that looked like Rankin dragged its prey down the hallway, seemingly oblivious to the cells on either side. "Bring him to me," she whispered.

As she moved down the corridor, ever closer to Raven's cell, the Aswang returned to her true form and shot out her barbed tongue, recoiling as it hit the glass instead of the woman behind it.

"Well, aren't you a feisty beast? I think I might like you."

The Aswang reached the cell and placed her hand on the cool surface, raking her long fingernails along the glass.

Raven stuck out her bottom lip in a pout and nodded in the direction of the panel beside her cell as she pointed at Givens.

Head tilted, the creature looked at the panel and saw how it looked like the one she had seen at the front of the building. She forced Givens onto his back and placed her weight on his chest before wrenching his arm free of its socket and slicing his throat wide open to silence his agonized wailing.

"That's my girl," Raven encouraged. "Let me out."

At the second attempt, the Aswang managed to get Givens' hand flush on the biometric panel. She stepped back as the glass door opened with a whoosh, and Raven stepped out into the corridor.

"Come, Silas," Raven called into her cell. A small, naked humanoid figure hopped off the bed and scuttled to her side, clinging to Raven's dress as he trembled with fear. Reaching down, she patted the top of his bald, horned head and whispered words of comfort. "Eat quickly, little one."

Silas leaped into the pool of blood spreading from Givens' neck and lapped at the still warm liquid. His distended belly moved in and out quickly as he drank, his penis growing harder with each swallow.

The Aswang's tongue shot towards Givens' prone form, but Raven deftly grabbed hold before it made contact, pulling the creature in close. "My little one eats first, but you shall get your turn. You've earned a reward and your freedom."

Raven reached out and snatched the severed arm out of the Aswang's hand, never breaking eye contact with the creature, whose black eyes had glossed over in a hypnotic trance. "Now you can eat. We shall be leaving soon, but I think I might need a few more helpers."

She moved down the corridor, looking into each of the cells as she passed. "Eenie meenie miney mo, which of you shall I let go?"

The imprisoned creatures threw themselves at the bars, sensing that they were about to be set free.

They behaved like animals at a shelter, putting on a show of affection and adoration for the one with the power to let them out.

Deciding on three more, Raven pressed Givens' hand against the biometric scanners of her chosen flock, making each of them kneel before her as they stepped out of their cells. "You are all mine now, and you will obey. Do you understand?"

They said nothing but kept their heads bowed in silent agreement.

"Arise, children, and let us take our leave. Silas, to me."

They all fell in line behind her as she strode down the hallway in the direction of the still open elevator. Just before she reached the exit, Rankin crawled out of the guard room, a tablet clutched to his chest. "Stop right there," he yelled.

"Or what, mortal?" Raven questioned, continuing to stride forward with purpose.

Rankin tapped at the tablet screen, gave it one final punch with his finger, and then smashed it to pieces on the floor. The overhead lights turned from white to red, and a siren began to wail, the sound sending the caged creatures into a frenzy.

"That's all you have?" Raven sighed. She raised her right hand and turned her index finger in a circular motion, watching with glee as Rankin's head turned one hundred and eighty degrees with a loud snap.

Raven and her motley crew of escapees stepped into the elevator. She placed Givens' hand on the scanner and used it to wave goodbye to her prison as the doors slid closed and the elevator began to climb.

Chapter Four

Drake passed through the security gate and walked briskly through the massive warehouse filled floor to ceiling with computer hardware. The building was a hive of activity, with employees driving forklift trucks and packing up orders set to go out to buyers from across the globe.

Thorn Industries was a massive organization, raking in billions of dollars every single year. Spenser Thorn had warehouses worldwide, but it was the Silicon Valley building that was the most special. None of the thousands of workers at the facility had any idea that there were monsters under their feet, and while they recognized Drake as a familiar face, they all assumed that he was private security for their boss.

That, in a sense, was true. Lionel Drake had initially taken the job with the belief that he would be heading up security for the Silicon Valley facility. Still, after a couple of months working closely with

Thorn, the finer details of his work became apparent. The minimum wage security guards at the building would answer to someone else, while Drake would be out in the field bagging werewolves, sasquatch, and other beasts ripped straight out of a horror novel.

Making his way to the back of the warehouse, Drake placed his hand on the biometric scanner and stepped through a doorway that led to a loading dock that opened up to a heavily guarded lot out back of the building. He could see the vans sitting outside, now seemingly empty, with Bits and Bytes nowhere in sight. He assumed that they had already left and were doing whatever they did to entertain themselves outside of their job.

A red light shone above the basement elevator, telling him that it was at the bottom of the shaft and not in use. Drake scanned his hand on the panel beside the elevator that led to Thorn's private office. The door opened immediately, and he stepped inside, thinking about how to explain the situation at the diner to his boss. He was positive that there was nothing to tie his team to the place, but he did not like leaving a mess behind during a job.

The elevator doors slid open, revealing an opulent lobby decorated with art pieces that probably cost more than Drake could even begin to fathom. An attractive brunette sat at a desk outside of Thorn's officing smiling at Drake as he stepped out of the elevator.

"I have a meeting with the boss, Janet."

"He is expecting you, Mister Drake. Please go right ahead."

Readjusting his backpack, Drake rapped on the heavy wooden door and stepped inside. He had been in the office countless times over the years, but it never failed to impress him. The dimly lit room looked like something torn out of an interior design magazine. Metallic shelves ran the length of the exposed brick walls. Skulls, horns, claws, and bone fragments were on display at every turn, some in glass cases, while others sat free. Recessed lighting highlighted the best of the pieces, casting shadows on the hardwood floor that stretched out and crept across the room.

Thorn sat behind his desk at the far end of the office space, his back to the room. He stared out the floor-to-ceiling windows, taking in the view of downtown off in the distance.

"Welcome, Lionel. Please help yourself to a drink and have a seat."

Drake glanced over at the extensive drinks cabinet and licked his lips at the prospect of downing a glass of overpriced Scotch. He fought the urge, though, and took a seat, dropping the backpack beside his chair. "I'm good for now, sir. Thank you."

"Always the professional." Thorn maneuvered his powerchair around to face Drake and moved in behind the desk. "Small talk first, or should we get straight to business?"

"I'm assuming you would like a brief rundown of how we caught the creature, sir?" Drake fought to maintain eye contact with his boss, even though doing so sent a shiver down his spine. Thorn looked perfectly normal on the right side, a handsome man with a hazel eye that always seemed to shine as though he were smiling. His skin looked tanned and youthful, and his brown hair was always nicely styled. His face's left side remained hidden under a mask that looked similar to *The Phantom of the Opera*, except that it was silver instead of white. His left eye never blinked, the lid torn away to reveal a milky white orb. Thorn had never seen under the mask and had no desire to. He also didn't know how Thorn had come to be that way, but rumor had it that he had gotten a little too close to one of his exhibits in the basement jail.

"Please. I'm interested to know what sort of fight she put up."

Drake cleared his throat and began to talk. "This was not a mission that went as planned, starting with the fact that we drove into the heart of an earthquake. By the time we got to the supposed resting spot of the asset, she was out and on the loose."

"The hospital?" Drake asked.

"You heard already?"

"I saw some reports on the news. They are calling it a killing spree by some madman, but it doesn't take a genius to put together what might have happened. Please, continue."

"Well, our tech told us that she was in there, but there were too many civilians in place for us to go storming in, guns blazing. We tracked her as she left, taking the form of a police officer. We believe that she may have infected him in some way to take control of his body."

"Infected how?"

"Ingestion of her blood would be my best guess. There was a big explosion at the hospital, and it looked as though one civilian was left standing after the blast. We watched on the scanner and saw it turn."

Reaching into his desk, Thorn removed a thick manila folder, which he flipped open and quickly studied. "There are a lot of legends

43

surrounding the Aswang, but this whole infection thing is something new to me."

"We are merely guessing here, sir. It could be something else entirely."

Thorn closed the folder and put it back in his desk drawer. "Plenty of time to study things in more detail now that we have her in captivity. Speaking of which, how did that go down?"

"We had our hand forced when the creature went crazy in a diner, attacking a pregnant woman with multiple witnesses in place. Unfortunately, the woman didn't make it, but Givens took care of the rest."

"He killed them?" Thorn asked, seemingly excited by the prospect.

"No, sir. Tranquilizers. I removed all the darts before we left, and I'm certain that no one in the diner got a decent look at us before Givens put them down."

"Security cameras?"

"None. This was a hole-in-the-wall diner, sir. Nothing fancy."

Drumming his fingers on the metallic plate covering one side of his face, Thorn went quiet for a moment.

"I can assure..."

"It's quite alright, Lionel. I have people in Los Angeles who can clean things up for us should anything unexpected arise."

Drake squirmed in his seat, knocking over the backpack beside his chair, which he had forgotten. "I do have one more thing, sir, that I believe you might enjoy?"

Eyebrow raised, Thorn watched with interest as Drake unzipped the bag and pulled out a bundle wrapped in an old flannel shirt. "What do we have here?"

Carefully unfolding the garment, Drake removed the infant Aswang and placed it face-up on the desk.

"Where did you find this little beauty?"

"It came out of the deceased pregnant woman. I think this is further proof that the Aswang can, I suppose, change those that she infects," Drake said.

"Indeed, but I do wonder why you are bringing it to me in this condition. That is, I assume, a bullet hole I see in the middle of its forehead."

Drake wiped his brow and shifted in his seat. "It was…I was angry. Had we acted sooner, that woman in the diner might still be alive."

"Well, besides the hole in its head, it seems to be in decent condition, although I am surprised that it is dead."

"How so, sir?"

"My research tells me that a bolo knife to the back is the only way to kill an Aswang." Thorn leaned in for a closer look and stuck his pinky finger in the bullet hole for a second. Wiggling it around, he watched for any sign of life, but when the creature remained still, he removed the digit and wiped it clean on the flannel shirt."

"Perhaps those turned by the creature are easier to kill."

"We'll get it to the lab and have the experts poke around. Let's see what they come up with, shall we?"

"Of course, sir."

"All in all, I would call this a successful mission. What about the new man? What was his name, Rankin was it?"

"Not such good news there. I had to incapacitate him before we captured the creature."

"Hmm. I had my doubts about that one, even though he came highly—" Thorn was interrupted mid-sentence as sirens began to wail. "What's happening?"

Drake leaped out of his chair, almost falling over it as he bounded for the office door, which flew open as Janet burst inside, a look of horror on her face. She pawed at his shirt as he ran past and headed for the elevator.

Inside the office, Thorn flipped open his laptop and brought up the security feed from the basement. He pulled the computer free of the charger, maneuvered around the desk, and raced after Drake, who was hammering at the elevator button. "It won't work," Thorn yelled.

"What are you talking about?"

"My personal elevator goes into lockdown in the event of a breach."

Glaring at his boss, Drake kicked at the elevator doors and screamed, "Override it, goddammit. I have people down there."

"If you mean Givens and Rankin, I can assure you that there is nothing left to save," Thorn said calmly. "I promise you that we are quite safe up here. That includes you, Janet."

Drake shook his head and tried to clear his thoughts. "You said breach. What do you mean by that?"

"I suppose you could call it a jailbreak."

"What got out?"

Tapping away at the laptop, Thorn accessed the security system and checked to see which of the cells were open. He turned pale as he took inventory.

Drake moved in and grabbed the handles of the powerchair, leaning down to get to eye-level with his employer. "What…got…OUT?"

"Raven," Thorn mumbled. "Raven and a few of her favorites."

Snatching up the laptop, Drake opened it and looked at the active screen. "Sweet Jesus. Override that fucking elevator and get me down there."

"Not until they leave, Lionel."

"We can't let those things just waltz out of here."

"We can, and we will. I know where Raven is going, and where she goes, she'll make her pets follow."

"Where?" Drake demanded.

"Round up a team. It's time to bring the girl in."

Chapter Five

Rebecca Grainger sat in the middle of the bedroom and tried to imagine what it would look like with a fresh lick of paint and some new furniture. For now, it was bare. Save for some garish floral wallpaper, which would be the first thing to go, and a bay window whose trim had seen better days. "This is going to take some work," she murmured.

"What was that?" her boyfriend Terry asked, tucking his smartphone into his pocket.

"Welcome back to the land of the living," Rebecca teased. "I said, we have some work ahead of us to make this room respectable."

"It's only a guest bedroom. I'm sure our friends will love that wallpaper. At least they don't have to sleep in a room with a creepy laundry chute in the wall."

"I don't see you complaining when you dump your filthy drawers down there," Rebecca said, nudging him playfully.

"True that. It's better than going down into the basement."

Rebecca reached up and tousled his curly brown hair. "My brave man. How would I ever live without you?"

"It's perfectly normal to be scared of dark basements. The sooner we can renovate down there, the better."

Pushing herself up off the floor, Rebecca stretched and padded over to the window. She looked down towards the bay and sighed contentedly. "I love this neighborhood. I still can't believe that my parents bought this house for us."

"I can't believe they bought the place right next to their own," Terry said, instantly regretting it.

Rebecca turned, her pale skin flushed almost as red as her hair. "I love that they are so close. Just because you had a shitty childhood and no relationship with your parents doesn't mean that I should abandon mine and move across the country."

"Baby, I'm sorry. I was poking fun. I love your parents and am so grateful that they bought us this place. We certainly couldn't afford it on our combined salaries."

Shoulders slumped, Rebecca walked over to her boyfriend and helped him to his feet, pulling him in for a hug. "I'm sorry I snapped. You know, I don't believe we have properly christened this room yet."

"I think you might be correct, lady," Terry growled as he nuzzled Rebecca's neck, raising a giggle.

She responded to his kisses, digging her nails into his back and pushing herself in tighter, loving the feel of his strong arms wrapped around her. Rebecca reached around and squeezed his ass, sliding her tongue into his mouth and kissing him hard.

DING DONG!!

The doorbell sounded impossibly loud in the empty room, but she ignored it as she began to pull Terry's T-shirt up over his head.

DING DONG!!

DING DONG!!

"They'll go away," Terry said.

DING DONG!!

Rebecca pulled free of his grip with a snarl and went to the window that looked down onto their front step. There she saw her mother standing with a casserole dish in her hand, preparing to ring the bell one more time. Rebecca rapped on the window and waved down to her mom to get her attention. "Okay, we may need to set some ground rules with that woman."

Fixing his shirt, which was halfway over his head, Terry slid down the wall with a moan.

"Don't you fret, my love, we'll pick up where we left off a little later." Rebecca skipped out of the room and turned back to blow her boyfriend a kiss. "You may want to cool down a little before you come downstairs. I don't need my mom seeing your assets on full display."

Putting on a happy face, Rebecca opened the front door. "Hey, Mom, this is a pleasant surprise."

Selina Grainger handed over the casserole dish and stepped inside, her eyes darting to every visible corner of the house. "I do hope I'm not interrupting."

"Not at all. We were trying to figure out what to do in, I mean, with the spare bedroom."

"You could leave it as-is for now and not do anything until you're ready to turn it into a nursery," Selina said with a wink.

Ignoring the comment, which she had already heard countless times, Rebecca said, "Where's Dad?"

"He'll be over in a moment. He's taking a phone call."

They walked through to the kitchen, where Rebecca placed the casserole dish on the counter. "What's for dinner?"

"Baked ziti. Pop it in the oven on low until your dad gets here."

54

Terry walked into the kitchen and placed a kiss on Selina's cheek. "To what do we owe the pleasure, Selina?"

Palms raised, she replied, "I know you kids are probably sick of the sight of myself and Craig, but we understand how tiring it can be to set up a new home. The least we can do is make you some dinner. Craig will bring a bottle of wine as soon as he gets off the damn phone."

"We love having you here, Mom, although a bit of notice would be good. Terry was about to decide what to eat when you showed up." She winked at her boyfriend, who was suddenly very interested in a piece of junk mail, his cheeks blazing red.

"I promise to call ahead next time, cross my heart," Selina said, making the sign of an X across her chest.

They sat at the dining room table and lapsed into comfortable conversation, the smell of the pasta filling the house. A few minutes later, the front door opened, and Craig stepped inside brandishing a bottle of wine and shouting 'knock knock' as he walked through to the dining room.

"Everything okay, dear?" Selina asked, a look of concern on her face.

"Not to alarm anyone, but we need to talk," Craig said.

"We can talk over dinner, Dad. I'm famished." Rebecca stood to go into the kitchen, but Craig caught hold of her wrist and held her in place. "What are you doing, Dad?"

"Please sit down, Becky. This is serious."

Selina stood and steered Rebecca back into her seat while staring down Craig. "What happened?"

"There's been an incident at the facility."

In the blink of an eye, Selina turned from doting mother into a fierce animal protecting its young. She pulled off the rubber band wrapped around her wrist and used it to tie back her hair. "Tell me more," she said, reaching down and retrieving a small pistol from an ankle holster.

"Is that a gun? What the hell is going on here?" Rebecca asked, a look of confusion on her face.

"Relax, dear," Selina said in a tone that said her words were more of an order than a suggestion.

"It's Raven," Craig said through gritted teeth.

"What about her?" Selina asked.

"She's out, and she has some company."

"Who the fuck is Raven?" Rebecca yelled.

Standing and checking to ensure that her weapon was loaded, Selina placed a hand on Rebecca's shoulder and said, "Your real mother. We need to get you somewhere safe."

"Thorn has men on the way. We stay put until they arrive."

Terry looked at each of the other people in the room and then glanced into the kitchen, where tendrils of smoke drifted out of the oven. "The baked ziti is burning," he said.

***

Raven stepped out of the elevator and into the lobby area, signaling the rest of the group to follow her. A chilly wind blew in through the open doors of the loading dock. It was the first time that outside air had touched her skin in twenty-five years, so she took a moment to savor it, throwing back her head and stretching out her arms. The wind washed over her, raising gooseflesh and blowing away the stink of years in captivity.

The moment passed quickly. It would serve them no good to stand around and wait for guards to arrive, which they almost certainly would soon. The alarm continued to sound, making her friends nervous. She turned and quieted them with soothing words that no human would have understood, words designed to soothe the most savage of beasts.

Raven strode over to the loading dock, tearing away the bottom part of her dress to make it easier to move. Catching sight of the cargo vans in the lot, she closed her eyes and began to speak quietly as she moved her thumbs back and forth across her fingers. She smiled as the sound of an engine coming to life reached her ears. Turning to face the group, she said, "Time to go, sweet ones."

The creatures edged forward and climbed into the back of the van, which was now back by the loading dock, engine idling and back doors wide open. Raven stopped the Aswang before it could climb into the vehicle, whispering in its ear. The creature took a step back and shuddered slightly as it took on the form of Rankin before jumping off the dock and into the driver's seat.

Turning to survey the lobby one more time, Raven tilted her head and stared at the elevator doors beside the one she had just used. She could smell Thorn and knew that the elevator led directly to him. The urge to find him and make him pay was strong, but she was weak. Using her powers after such a long time held in check was draining, but she promised herself that she would return and finish this piece of business as soon as her body and mind were strong enough to do so. With that, she jumped into the back of the van and leaned back to rest as the vehicle began to move.

Chapter Six

"What are you talking about, Mom?" Rebecca shrugged away Selina's hand and moved into the kitchen, where she pulled the smoking casserole dish out of the oven. She felt as though her world was spinning out of control and needed to do something that would make her feel grounded.

"We don't have time to explain everything right now. It's all about keeping you safe."

Rebecca slammed the dish down on the counter, hopping to the side as the lid flew off and clattered to the floor. "Dammit, Mom. What are you keeping me safe from?"

Craig moved away from the window in the living room and pulled a dishtowel out of the refrigerator door handle. He used it to pick up the glass lid, which he placed into the sink, before wiping up some pasta sauce from the counter where the casserole dish sat. "How about I give you a condensed version? We can explain the rest when we get to where we are going."

"Please," Rebecca said as she sat on Terry's lap, the only place where she felt safe.

Seating himself at the dining room table, he nodded in the direction of the living room window, which prompted Selina to go and take over the the street watch. "Where to begin?"

"How about by telling me who Raven is," Rebecca said.

"Raven is a witch, centuries-old, and also your mother."

"Okay, let's say I believe that, which may or may not be the case; you said that she got out. Was she in prison?"

"A prison of a sort." Craig sighed heavily and rubbed at his eyes with the heels of his hands. "There are things in this world that most people believe to be the stuff of legend. They are all real, and a good many of them are imprisoned here in San Francisco."

"Woah," Terry said, his eyes wide as saucers. "Are we talking some *Cabin in the Woods* shit here? I loved that movie."

Craig slammed his fists into the table and stared down Terry until the young man looked away. "This isn't some Hollywood bullshit, son, and the things that may be coming for your ass are not some actors who spent hours in a chair getting makeup slapped on. These things will fuck you up and enjoy doing it."

Terry blinked furiously. "I'm s-sorry," he stammered. "I don't know what's happening here."

"Then you had best shut your yapper and let me explain. But know one thing, son. Selina and I are here to protect this girl. You don't mean shit to us."

"Don't talk to him that way. He is going to be the father of…" Rebecca covered her mouth before the rest of the sentence escaped. The room fell into silence, all eyes on her as she tried to think of a way to take back the words that had just slipped out.

"You're pregnant?" Terry asked. "Why didn't you tell me?"

"I'm sorry, baby. I don't know for sure yet. I took a home test that looked like it was positive. I have an appointment with my doctor in a couple of days, but I guess I've already convinced myself that I am."

Pulling her in close, Terry hugged her hard. "I love you."

They jumped and broke the hug as Craig pounded on the dining room table again.

"What is wrong with you?" Rebecca asked. "And who are you if you are not my dad?"

"Selina and I aren't married, and we aren't your parents, but we feel like a family after all this time. We do love you like a daughter, but the truth is that we work for a man named Spencer Thorn."

"The billionaire computer guy?" Terry asked.

"Computer guy and collector of monsters. Plus, he owns this whole subdivision. Everyone who lives here works for Thorn in some capacity or another, but that doesn't matter right now."

"It matters to me," Rebecca said.

"I understand, but that little nugget you just shared complicates things."

"How so?"

"When your mother escaped, she took a few other inmates with her, including one that loves to feast on pregnant women and children."

Rebecca gripped the table, knuckles turning white, and tried to stop the room from spinning. "That's not funny."

"Do I look like I'm joking?"

"Wait," Terry said. "Are you telling us that those things are coming here? How would they know where we are?"

"Yeah, how would they?" Rebecca asked.

"Trust me, Becky, if your mother wants to find you, she will."

"I'm not sure why she would want to."

"Because you are probably more powerful than she is."

Rebecca laughed. "I don't have any special powers. Heck, I need Terry to open jars for me."

"Trust me. They are in there, and she will find a way to bring them out."

***

The van tore through the security gate and drove off into the night, weaving on the road as the wheels fought for purchase. Raven moved through the cramped space in the rear of the van and tore a ragged hole in the makeshift cage built into the hold. Just beyond the cage, on either side of the vehicle, were a pair of racks holding all manner of weapons. "Mortals and their pathetic little toys," she murmured as she slipped through the gap and into the passenger seat.

The vehicle was on the highway now, heading towards the city off in the distance. Raven peered back into the hold at the creatures packed in there. She knew that hiding in plain sight would not be an issue for her, but not so much for her new friends. They needed somewhere to hold up while her strength returned, but where?

Raven looked beyond the city skyline and saw some lights twinkling off in the distance, seemingly hovering above the water. She pointed at it and said, "Go there. I need to see what that is."

The van sped along the highway, moving smoothly in and out of traffic. With each passing mile, the lights shone brighter, and a structure built upon a rock in the middle of the bay came into clearer view.

"Yes. That is where we need to be. Go."

They drove on in silence, eventually reaching downtown San Francisco and the crowds converged around Fisherman's Wharf. Raven looked out across the water at the island, which was so close, yet so seemingly far away. Scanning the road ahead, she pointed to an access street off the main road. It led down to a smaller pier, where a couple of boats bobbed up and down in the water.

The Aswang, who was still donning Rankin's image, backed the van down the narrow thoroughfare and arrived at the dock. An older man watched the arrival of the vehicle warily as he hosed down his boat, wondering why it would be in a place that rarely saw any traffic.

Raven stepped out of the vehicle and approached the man, a smile painted on her face. "Hi there," she said, waving as she walked.

The old man looked around, believing that someone that beautiful had to be talking to someone else, but he was the only other person on the dock. "Can I help you?" he asked.

"We need to go there," Raven said, pointing out across the water. "Will you take us?"

"You want to go to Alcatraz? Lady, there are tour boats that will take you, but I'm afraid you're out of luck."

"Why is that?" Raven asked, touching the old man on the shoulder and giving a little squeeze.

"Well, it's closed for one thing. It's going to be that way for another couple of weeks while they perform some maintenance or upkeep shit. For another, our boats aren't allowed to dock there."

"Well, that sounds like good news to me. We'll have the place all to ourselves. Wouldn't you like that? I'd be more than happy to reward you."

The old man was very aware of the hand on his shoulder and the fingernails digging into the flesh beneath his shirt. The spot where she touched him felt warm, and he enjoyed the sensation of the heat now flowing through his body. "I-I'm not sure."

Raven leaned in close, her breath tickling his ear. "Of course, you are. You would love to take us there."

The old man nodded. "Yes. Yes, I would."

"What is your name?"

"Charlie."

"Good. Now, Charlie, my friends are going to come on your boat, but I need you to stay calm."

He nodded dreamily, the smallest of smiles touching the corners of his lips as the creatures marched past him and onto the boat. "What are they?" he asked.

"Never you mind, dearest Charlie. Take us to our destination."

The boat cut through the choppy water with ease and, within a matter of minutes, was pulling up to the dock at Alcatraz. Charlie looked at the group assembled in his boat and said, "One of you needs to take those ropes and tie us off."

Raven hopped off the boat as it glided up to the dock, tying the ropes and securing their craft. As she was about to step back on and take care of Charlie, she heard someone shouting off in the distance. Turning towards the sound, she saw a man running down the hill leading to the dock, waving a flashlight and looking less than pleased.

He was gasping for breath by the time he reached the dock, large sweat stains spreading from under his armpits. His pants, which were much too short, were held in place by a belt that strained at the buckle as it tried to hold back the massive belly trying to break loose. "You can't be here," he gasped. "We are closed."

"Who are you?" Raven asked indignantly.

"Security. I…"

"How many of you are here watching this place?"

The man opened his mouth to chastise the woman, but the words he wanted to say refused to come. Instead, he said, "Three. There are three of us, no more, no less."

"Thank you." Raven looked at the man, clapped her hands, and dodged the spray of blood that flew her way as his skull caved in. She pointed at one of the creatures in the boat and said, "You, find the others and take care of them."

The pale humanoid figure dropped down on all fours and sped past her, tearing up the hill and into the darkness.

Raven closed her eyes and sniffed at the air, her head moving slowly from side to side. After a moment, her eyelids fluttered open, and she pointed towards the city, a trail of green light emerging from her fingertips. "Charlie, you will take Silas back with you, do you understand?"

The old man nodded as though in a trance.

"My beloved Silas. Follow the path I have created for you and get my daughter. Charlie will bring you back when you have her."

The little imp hopped up and down excitedly, eager to make the witch happy.

Raven watched as the boat slipped away and headed back to shore, the sounds of agonized screams carrying across the rock as the Rake did her bidding. She turned and looked out across the Pacific as the fog began to roll in. The mist started to move faster as she sucked in her breath, pulling it closer to their new home and blanketing the area until it became impossible to see more than a couple of feet into the distance. She turned and exhaled, pushing the fog towards the city and providing cover for Silas as he began his mission.

Fully spent now, Raven felt her knees give out from under her. The Aswang caught her as she fell, holding her upright and leading her to the main building on Alcatraz. "Thank you, sweet one. Let us rest, and then we can get to work."

Chapter Seven

Selina stepped away from the living room window, a look of concern etched on her face. "Craig, have you heard any more from Thorn?"

"Nothing. Why?"

Motioning him over to the window, Selina pulled the curtain aside. "Look at the fog."

"It's San Francisco, Selina. Fog is rather common."

"Would you just look at it?"

Craig peered out the window, watching as the mist rolled past. Nothing looked out of the ordinary right away, but the more he looked, the more he began to see shapes form in the fog. It looked as though fingers were starting to form as it drifted past, each one pointing at the house before folding in on themselves. He went to pull the curtains closed, but Rebecca stopped him.

"Let me see," she said.

Stepping aside, Craig made space for her at the window, keeping an eye on the street, as much of it as he could see, looking for any sign of movement.

"What do you think is causing that light?" Rebecca asked.

"What light?"

"The green one. It looks like someone is shooting a laser pointer down the street."

They all crowded around the window, staring at the rolling fog but seeing no light.

"There's nothing but fog, baby," Terry said.

"You are telling me you can't see that light? Are you blind? It's pointing directly at the house."

Terry squinted and looked again but shook his head. "I'm not seeing it."

Pulling the curtains closed, Craig shepherded the group back to the dining room table. "Let's all just sit here and wait until our people arrive. It should be any time now."

As if on cue, Craig's smartphone began to vibrate, rattling against the wooden table. He snatched it up and took the call, nodding for a second before ending the call without ever saying a word. "They are five minutes out. Be ready to move."

THUMP!!

Something heavy hit the front door, causing everyone at the table to jump. Selina was the first to move, running to the bottom of the stairs, weapon raised and pointing at the door. "Get her upstairs. NOW."

Grabbing a handful of Rebecca's shirt, Craig pulled her off the chair and half-dragged her to the foot of the stairs. Turning back, he saw Terry still sitting at the table. "Are you coming, or should I put you out of your misery now?"

That seemed to do the trick. Terry crouched low and scampered to the stairs, following Craig and Rebecca up to the master bedroom.

"Stay in here and do not come out until I tell you to," Craig said as he pulled the door closed.

While Terry sat on the bed looking dazed and confused, Rebecca went to the window and looked up and down the street. The fog was so thick now that the houses across the way were little more than shadows, the swirling mist making it look as though they were moving, advancing on Rebecca's home like Lovecraftian terrors risen from the deep. If Craig and Selina were telling the truth, then monsters might indeed be real.

Rebecca angled her head so that she could see down to the front door. The outside light was on, but she could see nothing out there that might have been responsible for the banging on the door. She moved to the bedroom door and cracked it open, only to see Craig standing at the top of the stairs, gun in hand. He hissed at her and motioned at her to close the door.

Moving to the bed, she sat down beside her boyfriend and placed an arm around his shoulders. "Are you buying any of this?" she asked.

"Why would they lie, babe?"

"You really think I have some magical powers that I've been hiding since birth?"

Terry shrugged, refusing to make eye contact as he spoke. "I don't know about that part, but the monster collection thing freaks me out." He eventually lifted his head and looked at Rebecca. "What about you? Did you ever doubt that they were anything other than your parents?"

"Hell no. They have always been loving and supportive, not just to me but to each other. It makes no sense. They say that they gave up the last twenty-five years of their lives to babysit me. Why would anyone do that?"

"Thorn. That's a man with more money than sense if you ask me. If he owns this entire neighborhood, then he probably owns the people, too."

THUMP.

Rebecca almost tripped as she pushed away from the bed and went back to the window. She pressed her forehead against the glass and shielded her eyes with her hands, trying desperately to see through the fog.

"Is something out there?" Terry asked.

"Nothing that I can see."

THUMP.

"Babe, that's coming from inside the house," Terry said, pushing himself back on the bed and further away from the door.

"Oh, to hell with all this," Rebecca yelled as she charged across the bedroom and out into the hallway. The first thing she noticed was that Craig was gone. Peering over the railing, she saw Selina still crouched at the front door, gun pointed at the door. "Where's Craig?"

"Basement. Get back in your room, please."

THUMP THUMP.

THUMP THUMP.

"Selina, that noise is coming from inside the house."

"We know. That's why your father is in the basement. Get back inside and close that door. Help is almost here."

Catching movement out the corner of her eye, Rebecca turned just in time to see the door to the laundry chute pop open. A pair of tiny hands appeared at the top of the door, followed by a horned head. Rebecca screamed, causing the bedroom floor to shake, as the imp pulled itself free of the chute and ran at her.

It made it a couple of steps, its large flaccid penis flopping from side to side as it ran, before Terry grabbed it by the tail and halted its progress. The imp let out a frustrated scream as it flailed at the air, trying to get at its attacker.

"What should I do with it?" Terry wailed.

"Throw it back down the laundry chute."

Enraged, the imp twisted its body at an unnatural angle and sank its teeth into Terry's hand. It was enough to loosen the grip on its tail, and once free, it clambered up Terry's arm, teeth bared and ready to clamp down on his neck.

"Get off him, you fucking FREEEEEEAAAAAAAK." As she screamed,

Rebecca felt everything around her begin to slow down. The pitch of her voice changed until her high-pitched scream turned into a low, rumbling drone. She watched as the walls began to move outward, as though the house was exhaling slowly. The movement of the imp was down to a crawl as time thought about ceasing to exist.

Rebecca expected to feel as though she were moving in a dream, but she could function normally. As she tried to adjust to the sensation, the house inhaled, and the window shattered, sending shards of glass flying into the room. She watched as the pieces drifted lazily through the air, heading in her direction. Stepping forward, she selected the largest, sharpest piece and brushed the rest to the floor.

The imp was still making its slow ascent up Terry's arm, its leathery skin glistening with sweat. Rebecca reached out and pulled on one of its horns, exposing the devil's neck. Focusing on the flesh, she could see the carotid artery rise up, could sense the blood running through it. She flipped the shard of glass in her hand and slashed downward, the sharp end tearing through the exposed artery with ease. Blood leaked out through the wound, the droplets floating out like liquid let loose in zero gravity.

A loud creaking noise filled the room, and for a moment, Rebecca thought that the house was collapsing in on itself. The sound, though, came from the door to the room opening at the slowed-down pace of the world around her. "Enough," she whispered.

Rebecca fell to her knees as time caught up with her, the blood from the imp's neck splashing against her face on the way down. The creature fell beside her, clutching at its throat as it struggled to breathe. She looked at it and could see its wretched life play out in her head. She also sensed that it meant no harm, which was confusing to her.

"Rebecca. What happened?" Selina said as she burst through the bedroom door.

Ignoring the question, Rebecca looked the imp in the eye and smiled. "Goodnight, sweet Silas," she said as she plunged the shard of glass into its chest. "No more pain."

Footsteps thundered out in the hallway as the rescue team, led by Lionel Drake, ran into the house. Drake forced his way into the room and tried to help Rebecca to her feet.

"Get your fucking hands off me," she spat.

Drake surveyed the damage in the room and stepped back, hands raised in surrender. "I'm only trying to help, ma'am."

"You want to know how you can help?"

"Whatever you need."

"Take me to my father."

Craig stepped forward and held out his hand. "I'm right here, honey."

Rebecca stared him down with a look of disgust. "I said, my father. Take me to Spencer Thorn."

***

Raven tossed and turned in the bunk, sweat falling off her in waves. She clutched at her neck, feeling a jolt of pain pulse out from under her skin. Eyes fluttering, she sat up in the bunk and gagged, the coppery taste of blood caught in the back of her throat. "Silas," she whispered.

Leaning over the side of the bunk, Raven hacked and coughed and then shrieked as pain, sharp as a thousand razor blades dragged across her flesh all at once, hit her in the chest.

When the agony passed, she opened her eyes and said, "Rebecca."

Chapter Eight

Rebecca stared out the window of the SUV and ignored all attempts to engage her in conversation. Terry wasn't saying much of anything, maybe because he was in shock or perhaps because Rebecca has refused to clean up the blood splattered on her face. Selina and Craig had tried their best to console her, but she didn't feel as though she could trust them. Her whole life felt like a lie, and reconciling all of that could not begin until she got some answers from Thorn.

She watched the world fly by as they sped along the highway, their vehicle leading a small convoy of vans and trucks, trying to think about what she would say to the man she now knew to be her father. Would she feel sympathy for him or some strange connection, or would she rage at him, perhaps unleashing another round of powers that she now knew were inside her?

"We are about five minutes out," Drake called to no one in particular.

Shifting in her seat, Rebecca looked at the man sitting up front in the passenger seat. He had introduced himself as the head of security for Thorn Industries, but she thought he looked more like a trashy European villain from a cheesy eighties action movie. It was the unshaven look, the sunglasses at night, and the designer shirt opened one button further than necessary that made Rebecca feel that way.

Feeling her eyes boring a hole into his skull, Drake turned around and said, "Everyone okay back there?"

Craig and Selina, who sat in the middle row, both flashed a thumbs up while Terry mumbled something unintelligible. Rebecca continued to stare, trying to get inside Drake's head the way she had done with Silas. Nothing happened, though, so she turned away and looked out the window again, angry at herself for not being able to penetrate the man's thoughts.

The SUV slowed as it approached the ruined security gate, which was now guarded by a trio of personnel armed to the gills. Drake flashed his identification and briefly spoke to one of the men before the vehicle sped up again and headed for the massive warehouse up ahead. They passed through another security gate and pulled into a parking lot in front of a loading dock.

Rebecca was a little surprised at the final stop. She had imagined that they would be meeting Thorn at some mega-mansion overlooking the Pacific Ocean, not a warehouse where they made memory cards and motherboards. She stepped out into the night air and shrugged off Drake as he tried to help her out of the vehicle. "I've told you all already. No one, and I mean no one, but Terry gets to put their hand on me. Are we clear?"

Bowing slightly, Drake took a step back, pulling off his sunglasses and tucking them into the pocket of his shirt. "Crystal. If you would care to follow me, I'll show you to Mister Thorn's office."

They fell in line behind Drake and followed him up a set of stairs in the loading dock that led into the lobby that housed the elevators. One of them sat with the doors open, a pair of men in hazmat suits scrubbing down the interior.

"Is that an arm sticking out of that bucket?" Terry asked, aghast.

Drake doubled back and took Terry by the elbow, leading him away from the open elevator. "Nothing for you to worry about, sir. Please, come with me."

The doors to the other elevator slid open as soon as Drake placed his palm on the scanner. They all stepped inside and moved to the back, save for Drake, who held the door open with his foot.

"What are you doing?" Rebecca asked impatiently.

"We have two more coming."

He stepped back as a pair of men, who could have passed as brothers, stepped into the elevator, laptop bags slung over their shoulders.

"Who are these guys?" Rebecca asked.

"This would be our IT specialists Bits and Bytes."

Throwing her head back, Rebecca laughed and shook her head. "Unbelievable. We've just shifted from a horror movie into a James Bond flick. How cool."

"Don't be rude, Becky," Selina barked.

"Let it go," Craig chimed in.

Glaring at the woman that she had believed was her mother for the past quarter-century, Rebecca fought the urge to vent her anger and frustration. Closing her eyes and exhaling, she said, "You're right. I apologize. Nice to meet you both, Bits and Bytes."

The men nodded and then stepped out into the lobby outside Thorn's office, walking briskly to

Janet's now unoccupied desk, where they began setting up their laptops.

"Please wait here a moment," Drake said as he knocked on the office door and stepped inside.

Rebecca moved around the room, taking in some of the artifacts on display but mostly trying to keep an eye on what the computer guys were up to at the desk. She trusted no one but Terry, and her heart sank a little as she saw him slumped in a chair, looking confused and scared. She went to him and sat at his feet, taking his hands, which hung loosely by his side. "Are you hanging in there, my love?"

"Why didn't you wash your face?"

"Huh?"

"So much blood. I-I don't even know how you got that thing off me, let alone how you killed it. How can that be? I was there with you. Why don't I know what happened?"

Rebecca kissed his hands and then leaned in and kissed his forehead. "It was all so fast, but it felt super slow to me. I can't adequately explain it, but something happened to me back there."

"I don't understand."

"You don't need to right now. Just know that I am always going to protect you. No person or thing is ever going to get near you again. You got it?"

He smiled, but his eyes remained soulless and dead looking. "Can you please wash your face?"

"I will, I promise, but I need Thorn to see what I did to one of his precious museum pieces."

The office door opened, and Drake stepped out. "Mister Thorn will see you now, Miss Grainger."

Rebecca stood and helped Terry to his feet. "Let's go talk to this psycho."

"Just you, Miss Grainger."

"I'm not going anywhere without him," she barked.

"Please. No harm is going to come to Terry while we are here. Craig and Selina will look after him while you have a chat with Mister Thorn."

"It's okay," Terry mumbled.

Planting another kiss on his forehead, Rebecca marched into the office, muttering "asshole" to Drake as she blew past him. She made a beeline for the desk and sat down, waiting for Thorn to turn around.

The billionaire stared out the window, watching the woman's reflection as she entered his office. It was amazing how much she looked like her mother, and from the brief report he had received from Drake, her powers were just as strong, maybe even more so. He turned his powerchair and smiled at the woman sitting across from him. "Good evening, Miss Grainger, or may I call you Rebecca?"

"You may not."

"Miss Grainger it is then. Can I offer you a drink or perhaps a wet wipe for your face? That blood is rather jarring."

"You are seriously going to look at me with that mug of yours and talk about how I look?" Rebecca shot back.

"Touche."

"I have questions."

"I'm sure you do, and I am happy to answer them all." Thorn opened the desk drawer and pulled out a stack of folders, which he placed next to the laptop in front of him. "I have been prepared for your visit for quite some time. We have, as I am sure you now know, been keeping an eye on you."

"Maybe I will take that drink," Rebecca said. "And a washcloth."

"What's your poison, dear?"

"Gin and tonic."

Thorn snapped his fingers and pointed at the cabinet holding the alcohol. "An iced water for me, Lionel, if you don't mind."

Rebecca watched as the security man poured the drinks and then headed to the private bathroom attached to the office. He handed Rebecca a damp cloth before delivering their drinks and moving back to his spot by the office door.

"A security guard and a personal bartender all rolled into one. You must be paying him well," Rebecca said.

"Lionel makes out just fine. Now, questions, let me hear them."

After wiping her face and placing the soiled cloth on the corner of the desk, Rebecca picked up her drink and ran her finger around the rim of the glass. "Where was I born?"

"In a separate facility on these grounds."

"Why was I allowed to leave while Ag…my mother remained imprisoned?"

Thorn steepled his fingers and tapped them against his chin. "How can I put this delicately? We perform certain experiments here. Now, some might claim that doing these things makes me as much of a monster as the things I collect, but I am not without compassion and mercy. You were a precious, innocent baby. My experiment with you was all about nurture versus nature."

"How so?"

"Simple, really. If I had left you in the care of your mother, I do not doubt that you would have become just like her, powers and all. The exciting thing for me, though, was to watch how you would develop naturally."

Swallowing down the gin in a single shot, Rebecca slid the empty glass across the desk. "Can you have your lackey pour me another, please and thank you?"

Without prompt, Drake retrieved the empty glass and went to refill it.

"Are you sure that this was an experiment or were you simply worried that your seed would produce an unspectacular child?"

Blood rushed to Thorn's face. Rebecca could not tell whether it was from shame or anger, but she got a kick out of the reaction.

"It seems I struck a nerve."

Clearing his throat, Thorn regained some of his composure. "You seem to be suggesting that I am your father. Whatever would make you think that?"

"Silas showed me before he bled out like a stuck pig on my bedroom floor."

Throwing his head back as though struck on the chin, Thorn's eyes went wide. "How did he manage that?"

"I'm asking the questions, Daddy. How did my mother escape?"

"It was all caught on surveillance cameras. Lionel will show it to you once we are finished here."

"Two more questions, and then we can wrap this up. What else got out with her, and how are you planning on keeping my boyfriend and I safe until you round them all up again?"

Thorn flipped the laptop around so that it was facing Rebecca. "I would suggest that you can keep yourself safe at this point. I think you proved that tonight."

"I have no idea how I did what I did, though. It wasn't something I controlled."

"We can help you with that, help you harness your powers and learn how to use them to your advantage."

"Why would you do that?"

"Curiosity, for one thing. I want to know what powers you possess. Don't you want the same now that you've had a taste?"

It was Rebecca's turn to flush. She hated to agree with Thorn, but she had to admit that what she had done earlier that night had been as thrilling as it was terrifying. "Maybe I do," she confessed.

"I knew it." Thorn pumped his fist and smiled widely. "I should tell you, though, that I would also like your help in getting my creatures back. I feel like you owe me after killing one of them."

Drake reached over and placed the freshly refilled glass beside her. The piney scent of the gin tickled her nostrils and made her mouth water, but Rebecca resisted the urge to down the drink like she had the previous one.

"So, what do you think about my proposal?" Thorn asked.

"Tell me about the things that escaped."

Reaching over the top of the laptop, Thorn pressed a couple of keys and produced the image of a rail-thin humanoid creature with dark eyes. The picture showed it on all fours, mouth open as it appeared to scream at the photographer. He tossed the first of the folders over to Rebecca, who flipped it open. "The Rake. You may have heard of this one on the Creepypasta website. We planted the original story so that people would believe it to be nothing more than some urban legend, but he is quite real. He is also fast and prone to acts of violence, especially if it means getting a taste of human flesh. Our best guess is that Raven chose him as her personal attack dog."

Rebecca flipped through the file and felt her stomach turn as she came upon a series of pictures showing a group of armed men torn to pieces. "Jesus."

"Indeed. A tough one to capture." Thorn tapped the keyboard again and another image popped on the screen. This time, it was what looked to be an older woman whose flesh appeared to be melting off her body. It seemed as though she had talons on her hands and feet, all of which looked a good deal sharper than the shard of glass Rebecca had wielded earlier. "The Aswang. A shapeshifting creature that can become anything human that it touches. She was our newest addition, but she helped start the breakout before we could get her locked up."

Rebecca opened the folder that Thorn handed to her and shook her head. "This is crazy."

"She will help Raven get into places without too much commotion by shifting. It's how she got her out of here. Next up is the Nuckelavee."

The screen flipped to an image of a man on a horse, both of them missing their skin. Rebecca felt bile rise in her throat at the sight of the exposed bones and sinew. "That is grotesque."

"Yes, but also beautiful in a weird kind of way. The Nuckelavee does not like fresh water, but get him in the ocean, and he will get you where you want to go and quickly. A convenient friend to have when looking to make a quick escape by water. Raven chose her friends wisely."

"Is there more?" Rebecca asked, reaching for her glass.

"One more." Thorn tapped the keyboard one more time. "The Wenlutah. A wendigo/human hybrid native to one specific forest in Oregon. A ferocious meat eater, this thing will tear you apart and devour every scrap, bones and all."

Of all the creatures Thorn had shown her, the Wenlutah struck her as the most beautiful, albeit in a weird way. Its head looked like the skull of a massive antlered animal, and while it too was missing large chunks of flesh, its lean muscles were visually appealing. It had long arms and huge clawed hands, while its legs looked similar to those of a grasshopper.

"This is the only one that I consider to be disposable," Thorn said. "There is a herd of his brethren still roaming the forest, so catching another one should not be a problem."

Pushing the folders aside, Rebecca took a sip of her fresh drink and looked over the top of her glass at Thorn. "This all seems a bit much for someone who was teaching second graders a couple of days ago. I don't believe I'm up to the task."

"Is it a matter of money? The house is yours to keep, and I can deposit a sizeable amount of cash into your account and set things up to make it look like you won the lottery. Imagine, no more early mornings and days spent dealing with bratty, snot-nosed kids whose parents all look down on you."

"I'm happy with my life the way it is, snot-nosed kids and all."

"I see," Thorn said, nodding over in the direction of Drake.

"All I ask is that you keep us safe until those things are either dead or back behind bars."

"Plan B it is then," Thorn said, tapping at the laptop one more time. A live camera feed of a prison cell replaced the image of the Wenlutah. Terry gripped the bars and appeared to be yelling, but no sound came out of the speakers.

Rebecca leaped to her feet and pushed the laptop off the desk, taking satisfaction in the cracking sound it made as it hit the floor. She closed her eyes and let the rage build inside her, the heat of her anger spreading out through her body, all the way to the tips of her fingers and toes. She felt the floor begin to vibrate under her feet, watching as the items on the office shelves began to lift into the air.

Rebecca turned her attention to an animal skull with a single horn in the center of its head. She made it turn in the air until it was pointing directly at Thorn. Before she could launch it, though, she felt a hand on her shoulder and a pinching sensation in her neck. Her head lolled to one side, where Drake stood holding an empty syringe, arms outstretched, waiting to catch her as she fell.

Chapter Nine

Raven turned over in her bunk and stared out through the bars. It felt strange to be in prison again so soon after escaping one, but at least here, she was free to leave whenever she wanted.

Sitting up, she combed her fingers through her hair, pulling the bright red strands away from her face. The Rake, who stood guard outside her cell, dropped to all fours and turned to face her when he sensed movement. His chalk-white skin was dotted with red splotches, no doubt from the men he had hunted down the night before.

Across the way, the Aswang lay on her back, her arms dangling off either side of the bunk. Her chest rose and fell slowly, but Raven could tell that she was not asleep.

Trying to stand, Raven felt her legs give out again. She dropped to the bed with a groan and laid back down, placing her arm across her eyes. Weakness was not something she'd had to deal with very often in her long life, but using her powers after they had been dormant so long was taking a toll. She toyed with the idea of letting the fog roll away, but she also knew that it was necessary to keep it in place. As long as the island lay under a blanket of fog, Raven was sure that no others would come.

Patience was a virtue that she needed to learn if she hoped to reconnect with her daughter, especially now that Silas was gone. The vision of his death enraged Raven, but she was aware that Rebecca did not know his true nature until after killing the imp. The girl was protecting the one she loved, which Raven would also do to protect her new flock.

Leaving her arm over her eyes, she drifted away and thought back to the time when her life had changed forever.

***

Throughout her lifetime, which was centuries longer than she could remember, Raven had moved from place to place, never setting down roots and never making friends. Having friends would have meant explaining why she looked the same while everyone else withered and died.

It had been an interesting life, but also one that was fraught with danger at times. On more than one occasion, she had suffered accusations of witchcraft and had a death sentence by fire that she managed to evade by putting on a brutal display of her powers. That had come at a time when moving to the next town was not quite so simple as it was today. Raven had spent years in self-isolation, honing her powers to ensure that she would be able to fight off anyone that came for her.

It had all gone according to plan until she settled in San Francisco, setting up a small fortune teller shop on Pier 39. She quickly gained a reputation there, given that her readings and predictions were so accurate. Still, she also knew well enough to throw out some false statements so that clients would have enough junk information to believe that she might be just another charlatan.

Raven had gone unnoticed and had lived an ordinary life for so long that she let her guard down. She still practiced her form of magic daily in her readings, but the protective powers were set aside for so long that she couldn't call on them when the time came.

The day started as always, the vacation crowd wandering into her shop for a reading or to purchase other magic-related knick-knacks that she offered there. It was during a lull in the busy day that Thorn walked in. To Raven, he looked different than her usual clientele, which immediately made her a little nervous. Instead of the T-shirt, shorts, and flip-flops that were the standard uniform of holiday goers, the man looked like he had just stepped out of a business meeting.

He browsed the shelves for a moment and then sat at the small table set up in the middle of the room, on which sat a large crystal ball.

"Welcome to my lair, good sir. How might Madame Raven and her spirit guides serve you today?" Raven asked, laying on a thick Eastern European accent.

The man flipped a twenty-dollar bill on the table and flashed a smile that revealed blinding white teeth. "Well, I have been trying to locate something for quite some time, but it eludes me."

Raven waved her hands over the crystal ball, using a simple charm to make smoke billow inside. "I am being given clues to your name by my spirits. Please, do not tell me." Raven swayed from side to side, gazing into the crystal ball. "They are showing me a rose bush, but the flowers are wilted and dead. It is jagged and dangerous, just like you, Mister Thorn."

The man applauded and dropped another bill on the table. "That is very impressive. Now, what can you tell about the thing that I seek?"

Raven lowered her head and felt the skin on the back of her neck begin to prickle as another man walked into the shop. He closed the door behind him and flipped the sign from open to closed. "I sense that you are looking for a lost article of jewelry. A wedding ring perhaps," she said, feeding him nonsense.

"Are you trying to tell me that you do not sense that what I seek is sitting directly in front of me or that you are in immediate danger?"

Raven moved quickly, jumping up and pushing the table aside without ever laying a hand on it. The fast-moving piece of furniture knocked Thorn out of his chair and sent him to the ground, but it also opened a clear path for the other man in the shop. Before Raven could do anything else, she felt two sharp objects hit her in the chest. Stumbling backward, she fell into a book display and went down under the weight of it all coming down on her. Raven tried to stand, but the world around her spun until she blacked out.

She awoke to find herself naked and strapped to a metal table, unable to move or rid herself of the waves of cold washing over her body. One of the leather straps was pulled tight across her forehead, making it impossible to see around the room. Moving her eyes as far as possible to the left, she saw a metal IV pole beside her, a tube extending out and into her arm. Looking in the other direction, she saw Thorn lying on a table, nude but not held in place.

"You are awake, Raven. How splendid."

She tried to speak, but it felt as though there were cotton balls stuffed in her mouth. Tears of frustration spilled down her face as she tried to break free of the bonds. Numb and powerless, she wanted to scream, but nothing came.

Raven felt panic rise inside as a man in scrubs and a face mask appeared at her side, inserting a needle attached to a tube into the crook of her arm.

The insertion was little more than a feeling of slight pressure on her skin, but it felt like an invasion. She watched as the man moved over to Thorn and pushed a needle into his arm.

"You look frightened, dear. Don't be. This will all be over soon enough, and then you can go to the beautiful room that we have prepared for you."

Feeling some of the wooziness begin to melt away, Raven gritted her teeth and tried to summon her strength. The man in scrubs seemed to notice her efforts as he moved over to the IV pole and upped the dosage, sending fresh waves of icy cold through her body.

"We have some time to kill here while we perform this procedure. Would you like me to share what is happening with you?" Thorn asked.

Raven clenched her fists and tried to scream again.

Ignoring her apparent anger, Thorn began. "I have had my eye on you since before you landed in San Francisco. I knew of you when you were Clarissa in New Orleans and Beatrix in Savannah. You have done a fine job of covering your path through the ages, but when you have the money and means that I do, those covered tracks can very easily come to light."

Licking her lips, Raven managed to whisper, "You know nothing of my power. If you did, you would let me go now."

"I know everything there is to know about you, Raven, or should I call you by your given name? Baba Yaga?"

"Let me loose, and I shall spare you."

Thorn shook his head and tutted. "You are not going anywhere. You are about to become the best exhibit in my collection to date. You will also help make me all-powerful by donating a little of your blood to my cause. All of my guests make this donation so that soon I may become the most powerful being the world has ever seen."

Raven closed her eyes and blocked out the sound of Thorn's voice. She listened to the rush of blood pounding in her ears and imagined it warming her body from top to bottom. It took a moment, but the cold waves began to recede, replaced by a comfortable warmth that felt like a cozy blanket. The world around her slipped away until all that remained was the sound of the blood whooshing through her veins, growing warmer as it sped up. Sweat broke out all over her body as the blood grew warmer. "Boil," she whispered.

A blood-curdling scream snapped her out of the fugue state. Her skin, which was lobster red, began to return to its natural state, but on the other table, Thorn was burning from the inside out down one side.

"Get it out of me," he screamed. "Sweet Jesus, it burns."

The doctors removed the tube and clamped it, but not before a pool of blood gathered on the floor. Thorn went down into it face first, screaming again as the red-hot liquid seared the flesh off the side of his face and leaked into his eye socket, causing the eyeball to burst with a loud pop.

"Sedate that fucking bitch and spread her legs. DO IT NOW."

The coldness returned as the medicine coursed through her veins. Her eyelids drooped, but the doctors use spreaders to hold them open. Her eyes stung, the overhead light burning into her retinas. Thorn provided some relief as he stood over her and blocked out the light.

"Look at me, you cunt. Look at what you have done."

"So handsome," Raven slurred.

"You will never see the light of day again. I will banish you to a prison that I will make into a living hell. Your little plaything is already down there waiting for you. He is so very scared, as he should be."

"Silas," she gasped.

"It's an ugly child you have. How about we try to give you a pretty one? Would you like that?"

Raven tried to squirm, but the bonds and the sedatives removed all the fight. She stared into space as Thorn climbed on top of her, thinking of the ways she would kill him when she got the chance. The image of his being torn piece by piece calmed her as he grunted and moaned and had his way.

When he finished, Thorn removed the eyelid spreaders and leaned in close. "How did that feel? Did you like that, you fucking whore?"

Raven blinked furiously, trying to combat the feeling of sand spilled in her eyes. When she got the feeling back, she saw Thorn still on top of her and could feel him going limp inside her. "I can guarantee that your suffering will last a good deal longer than your pathetic fumblings."

Slapping her across the face with his good hand, Thorn climbed off and hissed as his burned foot made contact with the floor. With his anger now subsiding, the pain began to take him in its grip. "Help me," he said as the doctors lifted him onto a gurney and rushed him out of the room.

***

Dropping her arm to her side, Raven turned and looked out the cell, where the Rake sat, obedient as ever. She felt invigorated after her rest, although not yet strong enough to make a move. Raven thought about trying her magic with something small but feared that doing so would deplete her already tapped reserves.

One more day should do it. For now, it was all about building strength and thinking about how to repay Thorn for all the bad that he had done.

Chapter Ten

Rebecca sat up quickly and gripped the side of the bed as the room began to spin. Dropping her head, she pinched the bridge of her nose and tried to slow her breathing. The spinning started to abate, but she took a moment longer to allow it to pass fully.

The bed was unfamiliar, and the living quarters were cramped and bare save for the bed and a toilet. Rebecca tried to remember how she had landed here and groaned as it all came rushing back.

Rebecca jumped as a tapping sound filled the room. It was only then that she noticed that she was in a brick enclosure with a glass front. She peered out through the glass, still a little dizzy, and saw Selina there, rapping her nails on the clear surface.

"How are you feeling, dear?"

"Don't call me dear," Rebecca scoffed. "You are dead to me."

Shoulders drooping, Selina removed her hand from the glass and picked at a ragged nail on her thumb. "Please don't say that. You loved us up until a few hours ago."

"I did, but that was when I thought I knew who you were. You and Dad have been lying to me my entire life."

Selina smiled. "Still calling him Dad. That's a good sign."

"Force of habit. Don't get all excited."

"Becky, almost everything that we told you was the truth. Think of us as adoptive parents that didn't want to burden you with what we plucked you from."

"Do you love Craig?"

"What?"

"It's a simple question. Do you love him?"

Selina sighed and lifted herself out of the chair, looking down the long hallway of the prison. "In a way. It was all business at first, but as time passed, it began to feel as though we were a family. We all have needs, so sharing a bed and keeping up the pretense became easier over time."

The silence stretched on for a moment as Rebecca absorbed the answer. "It did feel real," she finally admitted.

"Your dad and I love you. That is something you need to believe."

"Hmm. Where is he now?"

"Craig? He's, uh, he's with Drake, taking Terry to a different location."

Rebecca stood and placed her hands against the glass. "Where? Where are they taking him? When can I see him? I need to know that he is alright."

"Thorn wouldn't tell me, but I'm sure he is being well looked after. Your dad may look as though he doesn't care much for your boyfriend, but he does. He won't let any harm come to Terry."

"What about me? Who's protecting me now?"

A bright light appeared at the end of the hallway before Selina could answer. Rebecca peered down the hallway to try and get a bead on what was happening. The light disappeared as the security door closed, and Thorn wheeled down the long corridor. The man knew how to make a grand entrance, stopping at several different cells to look in on his exhibits and offer encouraging words.

Finally, he arrived outside the glass enclosure, moving his powerchair beside Selina and reaching out to shake her hand. "Is our girl behaving?" he asked.

"She just woke up, Mister Thorn. She is worried about Terry."

"Tut tut, my dear. Terry will be fine as long as you play ball and help me retrieve my missing pets."

Rebecca fought to control her anger, not wanting to do anything that would put Terry in jeopardy. "I don't understand why you need me. Your people caught these things before, so surely they can do it again."

"That's a valid point, dear, but you must remember that when we caught them initially, we were taking them one at a time. This group scenario presents an issue. If this were a killing scenario, we could certainly take them out, but as I have already mentioned, I want them all back where they belong."

Pacing in the cell, Rebecca suddenly felt as though the walls were pressing in on her. All she wanted was to go back to her house with Terry, where the biggest problem was deciding which color to paint the spare bedroom. She had no idea how to call upon her powers, and even if she did, she worried that it wouldn't be enough to deliver what Thorn wanted. She turned to face her captor and said, "What guarantees do I have that you will allow me and Terry to walk away from this if I do what you want?"

"There are no guarantees in life, Miss Grainger, but I can tell you that I am a man of my word. I'm having Lionel take your boyfriend to a facility away from here, just in case Raven decides to return and come after me."

"Please, Rebecca," Selina said. "I've known this man for years. He has been nothing but good to our family."

Sitting on the stone floor, Rebecca sighed and looked down the long corridor at all the cells lined on both sides. Several pathways led away from the main thoroughfare, making her wonder how big this place was and how many creatures were in here with her. She considered asking but then decided that she didn't want to know. Being aware of the number might make her start thinking about how many other creatures were still running free. That type of thinking made the world feel a good deal less safe and not one into which she wanted to bring a child.

Rebecca stood and swiped at the butt of her jeans to remove any residue from the dusty floor. Her hand came away wet, and she panicked when she saw blood on her hand. "Oh, my God. My baby."

"There is no baby," Thorn said coldly. "Trust me; we tested to make sure. I'll have Selina bring you a change of clothes and some feminine products, and then we can begin."

"Begin what?"

"Pulling your powers out by hook or by crook."

***

The SUV rumbled slowly along the highway, keeping pace with the traffic, which was slower than usual due to the dense fog still blanketing the city. Drake sat behind the wheel, the beginnings of a headache tapping at his temples as he peered through the murky mist.

"I've never seen anything like this in all the time that I've lived here," Craig said.

"I thought fog was common here," Drake said, annoyed that his passenger was talking while he was trying to concentrate on the road.

"It is, but it usually blows out as quickly as it comes in. It never hangs around like this."

"I don't know what to tell you, pal. Mother Nature is weird."

They lapsed back into silence, which was a blessing to Drake. If he had to fill out a dating profile, he would describe himself as the strong silent type. That sounded better than the truth, which is that he would happily snap the neck of anyone who yapped at him for no good reason.

Ever since leaving the military, he had found it hard to find a group of friends like the ones he had in his squad. They all had his back no matter what. Civilians didn't understand the level of trust and respect required to make it as a soldier. Drake didn't have the words or patience to try explaining it, so he went the lone wolf route instead of constantly dealing with idiots. He groaned inwardly as Craig started talking again.

"I gotta tell you, man, I was as surprised as anyone when my daughter did what she did. Sure, she had a fiery temper, like any redhead, but she was usually gentle as a mouse. What is Raven like?"

"Are you asking if Rebecca has the same traits as her mother?"

"I guess."

Drake shrugged. "I don't know anything about her other than what I saw in the file. I wasn't in the picture when they nabbed her, but from what I can tell, she wasn't all bad."

"She was bad enough when she fucked up Rankin down in the hold."

"He probably had it coming," Drake mumbled.

Craig reached back between the seats and shook Terry, lying down in the back seat, eyes open and staring at nothing in particular. "Are you okay back there, kid? Do you need us to stop and get you a drink or a bite to eat?"

"We're not stopping—Thorn's orders. There will be plenty to eat and drink at the safe house. Just chill and enjoy the ride. It won't be much longer."

"I feel bad for him. I gave him a bit of a tough time when he started dating my daughter, but that's what fathers do, am I right?" Craig said.

Taking his attention off the road for a moment, Drake narrowed his eyes and said, "Craig, I swear to God, if you don't shut up, I am going to smack you in the fucking mouth. The girl is not your kid, and I don't know shit about being a dad. Drop it."

Crossing his arms and puffing out his cheeks, Craig turned his attention to the world outside the passenger window, which was now beginning to come into focus as they went beyond the city limits.

The remainder of the ride went by in silence as they turned off the highway and onto a set of rural roads free from traffic. Drake navigated the potholes easily, keeping the ride smooth until they turned onto a dirt road that had a rundown-looking house at the end.

"Is that place even habitable?" Craig asked before remembering that he was supposed to be quiet. "Sorry."

Drake pulled in front of the house and put the car in park. "I'm sorry I snapped. My head was pounding from trying to concentrate in that damn fog."

"Forget about it."

"And, yes, the house may not look like much from the outside, but it's cozy enough inside. Why don't you take the kid in and get him situated? I'll bring in the supplies."

Craig stepped out of the vehicle and stretched before opening the back door and giving Terry a shake. "Let's go, kid. I'll make us something to eat while you freshen up inside. What do you say?"

The young man slid out of the vehicle and stumbled as his feet hit the ground. Craig grabbed him around the waist and got him steady. They walked around the back of the car and went past

Drake, who was leaning inside the cargo area, moving stuff around.

As soon as they hit the steps of the front porch, Drake stood and pulled the gun out of his waistband. He took a couple of steps forward, braced his feet, and shot both men in the back of the head.

Pulling out his smartphone, Drake punched in Thorn's private number and waited for him to pick up, which he did on the third ring. "It's done. What do you want me to do now?"

"Hide the bodies and get back here as quickly as possible. Selina needs to go too. They all know too much."

"On it, sir. Sit tight; I won't be long."

Chapter Eleven

The police boat bobbed up and down in the water, the motion making the rookie feel a little sick. Officer Trey Mixon was already nervous about his first day on boat duty, but the vessel's movement was doing little to keep his burrito lunch where it belonged. He put his head down between his legs and breathed in deeply, fighting to keep the contents of his stomach at bay.

"You look a little green around the gills there, rookie. Do I need to fetch you a bucket?"

Trey sat up and swallowed hard, trying not to let his training officer see him in a moment of weakness. Sal Johnson was a veteran cop who did things his way and did little to hide the fact that he was not pleased about training another rookie, especially a black kid. He didn't do anything overtly racist, but Trey noticed the little things that Johnson said and did, things that he has experienced over and over again in the primarily white community where he lived. "I'm fine, sir. Thank you for asking."

"What about a life preserver? You need one of those?"

"No need, sir. I can swim."

Johnson raised his eyebrows as though surprised by the statement. "Good. One less thing for me to worry about."

The pilot stepped out of the boathouse and addressed his fellow officers. "Gentlemen, we will be pushing off in a couple of minutes. Our captain has overruled my objections to taking the boat out in this weather."

"Why the hell do they have us going to Alcatraz? It's closed down right now. Shit, the construction guys working there haven't been able to get onto the rock since this fog blew in."

"Tell me about it. Seems there are some security guys out there who haven't checked in for hours now. Probably just an issue with their communications, but the captain is friends with the guy who owns the security company, so we gotta go wet nurse these pricks."

"That's bullshit, Larry. You want me to operate the big light up front? Might help you see a little further ahead."

"Good idea. Hey, rookie. When I give you the order, untie us. You got it?"

"Yes, sir."

"Alright. Two minutes and we are good to go. If we don't hit something and sink to the bottom of the bay, I might just treat you fellas to a beer when we get back on dry land."

Trey winced at the comment and said a silent prayer. This was not how he expected his first visit to Alcatraz would go.

***

Construction lights lined the walls of the cellblock where Raven rested. They were dimly lit and didn't give off much of a glow, which was fine by her. She had grown accustomed to the half-light during her time and captivity and felt comforted by the familiar surroundings. Freedom was going to be more challenging to adjust to than she imagined, but once Thorn was out of the picture, Raven had a feeling things might go easier.

She closed her eyes and tried to imagine how her daughter looked now. She could sense her close by, but couldn't worm her way fully inside her head to get a clearer picture. Raven was concerned about Thorn and how much of his DNA had seeped into their child. She also worried that Thorn and his people might have corrupted her girl and told her things that were not true. She would just have to cross that bridge when the time came, but if they had messed with her child, there would be hell to pay.

Raven sat up as gooseflesh prickled her flesh. Danger was coming; she could feel it. She stepped out of her cell and placed a hand on the Rake's shoulder. "Go," she said, pointing at the exit to the prison. The creature bounded away on all fours, sniffing the air and gathering speed as he picked up a scent.

No sooner had he left the building than the Nuckelavee bounded in. The horse approached slowly and bent its front legs to get down to eye level with Raven. The rider leaned forward and spoke in a gruff Scottish accent. "Men are coming. Get on."

Raven grabbed onto his outstretched arm and allowed him to pull her onto the horse. The exposed bones of the horse and rider, who were fused together, dug at her skin, but now was not the time for complaints.

The rider stopped on the way out of the building and lifted a long piece of rebar, which he twirled like a baton. The metal made a swishing sound as it cut through the air. Happy with his weapon, the rider turned to Raven and said, "Hold on tight, lass."

They flew out of the building, the wind whipping through Raven's hair as they rode. Looking down towards the dock, she saw a vessel approaching, its bright light looking like the glowing eye of a sea monster as it breached the surface.

She was ready to fight, but with her familiars in place, Raven believed she might not need to.

***

"Keep that light on the dock, Sal, and hold on tight. I can't guarantee a perfect docking," Larry yelled from the boathouse.

Trey looked up at Alcatraz, but there was little to see. The high-powered light operated by Sal caught parts of the main building as the boat bobbed up and down, but they were nothing but fleeting glimpses of the structure.

Larry eased the boat into the dock, the sound of metal on metal tearing through the night as he got a little too close. "Tie it up, rookie."

Leaping onto the dock, rope in hand, Trey formed the best knot he could and hoped it would hold.

Sal jumped down beside him and patted him on the shoulder. "Good job not throwing up, kid. Let's find the security guys and get the hell out of here. This place gives me the willies."

The cops pulled out their flashlights and used them to guide themselves along the dock and up onto the prison's main landing area. They both almost screamed aloud when a large man stepped out of the mist, a big grin spread across his face.

"Sorry, officers, I didn't mean to startle you. What brings you to the rock?"

"It's a routine check-in, sir," Sal said, shining his light in the man's face and looking for signs of intoxication or drug use. "Your boss says he hasn't heard from you guys in a while."

Raising his hands and motioning at the sky, the security guard said, "We can't get through. Communications are down with this weather. You can let them know that we are right as rain here."

Sal nodded, but something felt off. It was the big man's eyes and how they reflected the light from his torch. "Makes sense. Where's the rest of your crew?"

The big man took a step back and to the side as he pointed up the hill. "We have a place up near the top. They're up there now having a bite to eat."

"You wouldn't have any coffee up there, would you? It's cold out there on the water, and I could use a little something to warm me up. You thirsty, rookie? You wanna come for a hike with me up to the guard station?"

"Sound good," Trey said, moving in beside his boss and getting the feeling that something was very off.

"Lead the way. Sorry, big fella, I didn't catch your name."

"It's Norman, but there's no need to follow me. My friends are coming to you."

Sal pulled out his weapon and pointed it at Norman, who was now trembling as his skin seemed to change with each movement. "Trey, get your ass down there and get that boat untied. We are leaving now. Norman, get your ass on the ground and put your hands behind your back."

Trey bolted for the dock, but he had barely taken three steps when something big and fast came out of the air and pinned him to the ground. The smell of rotting flesh hit him in the face, and this time he did lose his lunch as vomit flew from his mouth as he tried to scream.

"Get the fuck out of here, Larry," Sal yelled back to the boat as the Aswang and the Rake advanced on him. He unloaded his weapon, missing the targets with every shot, and fumbled in his utility belt for a fresh clip. He never got close, as his attackers took him down and mercifully ended his life quickly.

Trey scrambled backward, trying to evade the beast that was now toying with him. It would let him get a couple of feet away, but every time he tried to stand, it would hop forward on its weird hind legs and pin him down again. As it landed on him again, his flashlight rolled out of his hand, the beam of light resting on Sal, who had a pair of creatures feasting on his insides.

"What's happening up there?" Larry called out.

"GO," Trey screamed. "Save yourself and go."

Larry ran to the back of the boat and hopped onto the deck. He untied the rope, tossed it into the vessel, and went down hard as he slipped on the wet deck. Scrambling to his feet, he ran for the boathouse but stopped as he heard the sound of hooves on concrete. Looking into the fog, he saw a pair of what looked to be red lights approaching. It took his brain a moment to register that they were eyes. That was when Larry screamed.

***

The Nuckelavee picked up speed as it raced down to the waterfront, the rider now holding the rebar like he was about to joust a knight. Raven held on for dear life as they made the final turn and galloped across the landing area. She had a moment to see the Wenlutah snapping off the head of a cop in a single bite before the horse leaped and they flew through the air.

The rider leaned low and extended his arm, shifting the rebar a touch to the right. His measurements were inch-perfect as the metal flew into the open mouth of the screaming cop and out through the back of his head.

The Nuckelavee soared over the boat, the rider lifting the impaled officer as they cleared the vessel and plunged into the frigid water beyond. The horse navigated the water with ease, turning smoothly and heading back to the dock as the rider tossed the rebar and the attached cop into the depths.

They climbed out of the water and onto the dock in one graceful motion. Raven was cold and wet, but she couldn't remember a time in her life when she'd felt more alive. She jumped down off the Nuckelavee and shook herself like a dog. Walking around the landing area, she watched as her friends fed and knew that she had chosen well. She knew that they would give their lives to protect her, and she vowed that she would do the same for them.

Chapter Twelve

Rebecca stepped out of the vehicle and immediately felt self-conscious. The activewear that Selina had provided as a change of clothing was form-fitting and clung to her slender frame like a second skin. If anyone else noticed, they didn't let on. Drake walked ahead and held open the door to the building that sat a couple of miles up the road from the Thorn Industries main warehouse.

Bits and Bytes arrived in a second vehicle and walked past Rebecca without so much as a second glance. They were much too busy arguing over something on their target to notice the pretty redhead in the figure-hugging yoga pants. "Get a grip, Rebecca," she muttered to herself as she strode to the building and stepped inside.

She wasn't sure what to expect based on the building's bland exterior, but the inside looked like a place where elite warriors went to train. One half of the vast space was filled with exercise equipment, while the other side played host to all manner of targets and tackle dummies, many of which looked the worse for wear. A group of armed men circled the inside of the building while Bits and Bytes sat with Thorn looking at an array of computer screens.

Drake stepped in behind her and pulled the door closed. He gently touched her on the shoulder and pointed in the direction of Thorn, who was now looking their way.

"The prodigal daughter arrives," the billionaire said as he expertly guided his powerchair through the target practice area. "Are you ready to go to work?"

Rebecca looked around the space and nodded. "Yeah, whatever that means."

"It means, my dear, that we are going to prepare you for war by introducing you to the weapons that you have at your disposal."

"I still have no idea how that is going to happen."

"I think I might," Thorn said, tossing her a garment that looked like a sports bra with built-in speakers in front and back.

"What am I supposed to do with this?"

"You wear it, of course."

Eyeing the garment warily, Rebecca asked, "Is there somewhere a little more private where I can put this on."

"There is a locker room just beyond the gym, but please do hurry."

Rebecca jogged to the back of the facility and stepped into the trendiest-looking locker room she had ever seen. It was apparent that Thorn had spared no expense in setting the place up, which made her wonder just how big his security detail really was. She put on the sports bra and then slipped her T-shirt on over the top. The speaker-looking units on the garment dug into her skin, but a slight adjustment relieved the pressure.

She took a look at herself in the mirror and headed back out to the target area, where Thorn sat waiting for her.

"How does it feel on you?" he asked.

"Snug, but not too uncomfortable."

"Good, good."

"Now, do you care to explain what is going on and what it's for?"

Thorn guided himself back over to the computer table and tapped at one of the laptops.

Within a matter of seconds, Rebecca felt the garment begin to warm up. The heat was pleasant at first, but it quickly became painful. "Ouch. Turn it off. HOT."

Without looking up, Thorn tapped away at the keyboard and waited for a response.

The heat stopped almost immediately, but it gave way to a blast of cold that made Rebecca feel like she was soaking in an ice bath. It didn't hurt like the heat did, but she still wanted it gone.

"Embrace it," Thorn yelled from behind his computer.

Rebecca gritted her teeth, which were beginning to chatter, and tried to block out the cold. For a moment, it felt as though she had it under control, but the cold won out, dropping her to her knees as it penetrated her skin.

"Shut it down," Thorn said to Bits and Bytes as he guided his chair over to Rebecca.

"What are you doing?" she asked, her body shaking with the cold.

"Testing a theory. You made a comment about my face when we first met. How do you think it became that way?"

"How should I know? One of your animals attacked you?"

"Common guess, but only partially correct." Thorn reached up with his damaged hand and tugged at the metallic mask covering half his face. It came away easily, and he dropped it into his lap. "Look and tell me what you see."

Letting out a gasp, Rebecca looked upon his ruined face and knew that the damage did not come at the fang or claw of any animal. The flesh that remained looked like melted wax allowed to cool after the snuffing of a candle. "Were you in a fire?"

"No. I drew the ire of your mother."

"She did that to you? How?"

Thorn returned the mask to its rightful place and, for a second, looked afraid. "What I am about to tell you may sound like the ravings of an absolute psychopath, but it will also help explain what I am trying to do with you here."

With a nod, Rebecca urged him to tell the story.

"When I was a younger man, I became obsessed with the idea of power. My business had already taken off, and I was wealthy beyond my wildest dreams. They say that money is power, but that's not wholly accurate. Yes, it opened doors and allowed me to corrupt and cheat my way to the top.

When I reached that point, I realized that my idea of power was not what others believed it to be."

"You wanted magic," Rebecca said.

Snapping his fingers, Thorn pointed at her. "You get it. My collection was already growing at that time, but it was the Baba Yaga, your mother, that was my biggest, most elusive prize. Who would ever have believed that she would come to me? I took that as a sign."

"A sign of what exactly?"

"I have a little of all my creatures inside me. Their blood flows through my veins, yet I cannot do what they do. I believed that Raven's blood would be the catalyst that kick-started everything. I believed I would finally have the power I so desired."

"Raven didn't play ball?"

Thorn shook his head. "No. Strapped down and sedated, she found a way to boil her blood in the middle of a transfusion." He pointed to the mask. "This was the result. I was furious, and I took out my anger on her."

Rebecca took a step back and balled her fists. "You hurt her."

"I took her power in another way. That was the night you were conceived."

A loud hum filled the room, and the weights on the gym equipment began to rattle. Arms outstretched, Rebecca went up onto her tiptoes and lifted off the floor ever so slightly, heat coming off her in waves.

Thorn kept his eyes on her but pointed over to Bits and Bytes and signaled them with a light switch flicking motion. "Stop, Rebecca. Stop," he whispered.

She continued to float upward for a few more inches before collapsing to the floor, frozen breath escaping her lips. "What happened?" she asked.

"You controlled your power without knowing you were doing it. It's all about controlling your emotions. You got angry as I told you about your mother. While that was happening, Bits and

Bytes were cranking up the heat, just like we did a few minutes ago when you couldn't handle it."

"I didn't feel it."

"Your body adjusted. Think about words that people use when talking about being angry. Words like heated and steamed, unlike when you are scared, it's more like…"

"Frozen," Rebecca said.

"I believe that your body temperature generates your powers. Your job is to figure out what you can do in various states. We can regulate your body heat using that fantastic garment you're wearing under that shirt. You need to level it out and see what you can do at different temperatures."

"I think I get it."

"Let's test it out." Thorn pointed at an archery target in the far corner of the building. "Bullseye," he said.

Planting her feet on the floor, Rebecca looked over at Bits and Bytes and nodded at them to begin. She felt the heat begin to radiate out from the units on her chest and back, hissing as her skin began to blister. Staring down the target and getting the range, she closed her eyes and tuned in to the sound of her heart hammering. She imagined the sound to be a ticking time bomb seconds away from exploding. Allowing the device to explode in her mind's eyes, she sucked in the heat of the blast and then blew it outwards.

The security team in the building let out a collective gasp as bolts of light shot out of Rebecca's eyes, converging as one and tearing a hole through the center of the target.

"Bravo, my dear. Outstanding work."

Rebecca looked at her handiwork and felt equal parts excited and afraid.

"How did that feel?" Thorn asked. "Tell me everything."

"It felt natural. How long did it take me to do that?"

"A little over a second after we applied the heat."

"That can't be right. It felt much longer."

"Time might not work the same for you when you are in control."

The image of the incident with Silas back at the house flashed into her mind. "Yes, maybe. What's next?"

"How about we do some more until you get to a point where we don't need to use the heating and cooling elements?"

"Let's do it."

***

Raven had never had an issue with the ailments suffered by mortal folk, but the dip in the ocean seemed to be causing problems. She lay in bed and floated in and out of sleep, feeling feverish one moment and close to freezing the next.

The Rake sat on the floor beside her bed, ever vigilant. She held out her hand and placed it on his head, his cool skin soothing her as the fever hit again.

Closing her eyes, she whispered her daughter's name before sleep took her.

***

The building's target practice side sat in ruins. Targets and dummies pulled apart, the pieces scattered across the room. Rebecca stood in the middle of the maelstrom and surveyed what she had done. She had proven to be a quick learner and now had an arsenal of powers to call upon at any given time. Despite that, she still felt as though much more hid under the surface, just out of reach.

"I believe you are ready," Thorn said.

"When do we begin?"

"Tomorrow. We'll be taking a trip to Alcatraz."

"Why would we go there?"

"Because, my dear. That is where our merry band is hiding out."

Rebecca shook her head, confused. "How could you possibly know that?"

"When we caught the Wenlutah, we had the idea of chipping him and sending him back out with his tribe. We wanted to track their movements and feeding patterns from afar. He is still wearing that chip, and unless he learned how to swim, he had some help getting over there. That tells me that they are all still together."

Bits and Bytes interrupted the conversation, eyeing one another with smirks on their faces. It was Bytes who spoke up. "We have a suggestion."

"What's that?" Rebecca asked.

"We were impressed by your performance today and think you deserve a killer codename, just like we have."

Rebecca rolled her eyes and was about to shoot them down when a name popped into her head. "Okay, boys, you can call me Salem."

Salem will return in Salem Unleashed, coming in September.

Acknowledgments

After the disappointment of a failed *USA Today* list run, it was nice to get back to the business of writing. As always, a huge thank you to my wife Penny, who has somehow made it through my mood swings of the past couple of months during the run without killing me.

Thanks again to my PA, Diana Richie, for beta reading and for her help during the list run.

Thank you to Erin Lee and Crazy Ink for continuing to publish my work even when I miss a deadline. I promise to get better.

Finally, thank you to everyone who reads, reviews, and supports my work. I hope this one met your expectations.

Born under a gloomy, grey, Scottish sky, it is perhaps no real surprise that darkness has always felt comfortable to John Watson. After countless hours spent in his local library, he found that he was more at home in the worlds of Clive Barker, Stephen King, and James Herbert than he was in his own. The need to carve out his own niche in the horror genre drove Watson to slice open his mind and let the words spill onto the page.

From donuts to mysterious karaoke bars in the middle of nowhere, Watson mines the depths of the ordinary to find the evil that lurks beneath the surface. He dares you to join him in his ongoing forays into the dark side.

John Watson's Novels and Novellas

Karaoke Night

Crueller

Off the Grid

Be Kind, Rewind

Cradle Robber

Slave to Blood

Swimming Upstream

Anthologies

Infamy

Beyond the Jungle

Murder Maker

Follow John Watson

https://www.facebook.com/authorjohnwatson

Made in the USA
Monee, IL
17 April 2023